Ra
the
Mighty

CAT DETECTIVE

Ra
the
Mighty

❦ CAT ❧
DETECTIVE

BY

A. B. Greenfield

ILLUSTRATED BY

Sarah Horne

Holiday House 🐱 New York

HOLIDAY HOUSE is registered in the U.S. Patent and Trademark Office.
Printed and bound in June 2019 at Maple Press, York, PA, USA.
The artwork was created with pen and ink with a digital finish.
www.holidayhouse.com
3 5 7 9 10 8 6 4 2

Library of Congress Cataloging-in-Publication Data
Names: Greenfield, Amy Butler, 1968– author. | Horne, Sarah,
1979– illustrator.
Title: Ra the mighty / by A. B. Greenfield ; illustrations by Sarah Horne.
Description: First Edition. | New York : Holiday House, [2018] | Summary:
In ancient Egypt, the Pharaoh's pampered cat Ra and his scarab-beetle
sidekick question the royal palace's animal inhabitants, solve a crime,
and exonerate a servant girl falsely accused of theft.
Identifiers: LCCN 2017043190 | ISBN 9780823440276 (hardcover)
Subjects: | CYAC: Cats—Fiction. | Scarabs—Fiction. | Animals—Fiction.
Stealing—Fiction. | Egypt—History—To 332 B.C.—Fiction. | Mystery
and detective stories.
Classification: LCC PZ7.G8445 Rab 2018 | DDC [Fic]—dc23
LC record available at https://lccn.loc.gov/2017043190

ISBN: 978-0-8234-4438-0 (paperback)

For Tessa,
who knows the right way
to address a cat
—A. B. G.

CHAPTER I

Invasion

When my adventures began, crime was the last thing on my mind. Stretched out by Pharaoh's pool in the hot Egyptian sun, I was doing what I do best—absolutely nothing at all.

"Ra, you are the laziest creature I know," my friend Khepri said.

I ignored him. Khepri's a scarab beetle, so he's only about the size of my paw, and his voice is tiny. But when he crept closer to my ear and said it again, I yawned and half-opened my eyes.

"Lazy? Me?" I blinked. "Never, Khepri. I make the most of every hour."

"But you haven't moved a whisker all day," Khepri protested.

"That's the beauty of it, Khepri. I don't *need* to move. I'm already in the best place possible." I glanced over his shiny black wings and admired the calm water in the pool. "It's sunny, and it's peaceful. Even better, the people here treat me like a god. Believe me, I'm making the most of *that*."

Khepri flashed his wings. "Well, people think highly of me, too. There isn't a mummy in Egypt that doesn't have a scarab amulet over its heart. But I don't let that go to my head, Ra. I keep busy."

"Let me guess." I wrinkled my nose. "You've been rolling dung balls again."

"I have indeed." Khepri rubbed his forelegs. "First thing this morning, I started over by the stables—"

"I don't want to know the details, Khepri." Scarab beetles love dung, but Khepri loves it more than most. I tried to cover my ears with my paws, but it was no use.

"And you wouldn't believe how much dung I found there," Khepri went on. "Piles of it—"

"Stop," I moaned.

He did, but not because of me. A serving boy strode up with a midmorning snack. Khepri had to scurry back to avoid being stepped on.

With a deep bow, the boy set my plate down in front of me. I gave him a gracious nod, but I waited until he left before I nibbled at the offerings. Letting the humans watch you eat is always a mistake. It's hard to look like a god when you're wolfing down antelope stew.

I didn't mind Khepri seeing me, though. Compared with his meals, mine are classy in the extreme. After I had polished off all the morsels on my plate—not only antelope stew, but some tidbits of spiced ibex—I rolled onto my back with a happy sigh. "Delicious. I tell you, Khepri, the cooks here get better every day."

"And now what?' Khepri said. "You're going to lie around waiting for the next meal?"

"And what's wrong with that?"

"Ra, you need to get out more. I've known mummies with more interesting lives."

What kind of comparison was that? "Mummies don't eat," I pointed out. "Or sleep."

"There's more to life than eating and sleeping," Khepri said. "Not that anyone would know it, the way you act. Even when Pharaoh took you to Thebes last month, you didn't lift a paw. His servants carried you straight from this pool to the sunny deck of the ship. And then they carried you back."

I nuzzled my paws. "So what if they did?"

Khepri sighed. "Don't you get bored, Ra?"

"How can I be bored when there are snacks?" I said reasonably.

"You're hopeless," Khepri told me. "You've got less get-up-and-go than one of Pharaoh's wigs."

I rolled over and licked the last bit of gravy off the plate. Khepri could say what he liked, but I had plenty of get-up-and-go when I wanted to. I just didn't want to very often.

A few years ago, when Pharaoh was just a prince, it was different. I used to roam around then. But now I wasn't an ordinary palace cat. I was *Pharaoh's Cat*, and there was no need to gad about. Everything I wanted was right here.

And of course I didn't get bored.

Well, not very often, anyway. Only when my snack was done and it was hours and hours until the next one would arrive.

Like right now.

Not that I was going to mention it to Khepri. After all, I counted myself lucky I didn't have all the claims on my time that Pharaoh did—so many ambassadors to receive, so many rites to perform, and so much to live up to as he followed in his father's footsteps. None of that for me! As Pharaoh's Cat, my life was easier than ever. If I was a teensy bit bored sometimes, so what?

Anyway, if I complained, Khepri would invite me to roll dung balls with him. He doesn't seem to appreciate the dignity of my position.

Now that I'm Pharaoh's Cat, I live an exalted life, just as Pharaoh himself does. Everyone else in Egypt understands that. They generally show their respect; they keep their distance. But not Khepri.

Really, sometimes I don't know why I put up with him.

"Ra, it's not good for you to lie around all day like this," Khepri said now. "You need another interest in life."

"No, Khepri." I slouched back down beside the pool, rubbing one cheek against the tiles. "What I need is a nap."

Khepri drummed his forelegs in a marching beat. "You've slept plenty already. Let's get you moving."

"We can talk about it after my nap," I mumbled.

"Hey!" Khepri stopped drumming. "What was that?"

"I said—"

"Not you." Khepri hopped around and faced the high wall at the far end of the courtyard. "Over there. That scratching sound."

As I turned my head to listen, a cat popped over the wall.

I sat up.

Cats may be gods in Egypt, but I'd be the first to tell you that not all of us look the part. This one was a mess—young and scrawny with bedraggled fur and a torn ear. Definitely not the kind of cat who belonged in the palace, let alone in Pharaoh's private quarters.

"Hey, there!" Panting, she scrabbled over to me.

I drew myself up higher. *Hey, there?* What kind of greeting was that for Ra the Mighty, Lord of the Powerful Paw, direct descendant of the cat goddess Bastet and the great sun god Ra himself?

I flicked my right ear. "Excuse me? Have we met?"

"No," she said. "I'm Miu. I live by the kitchens. And I need your help."

Help sounded an awful lot like *work*. And why should I work for a creature who didn't even know the polite way to approach Pharaoh's Cat? I stretched myself out by the water. "Sorry. I'm busy."

The youngster leaped over me and lowered her face down to mine. "You don't look busy to me."

The nerve! Didn't she understand she needed to treat Pharaoh's Cat with respect? I put out a paw to ward her off. "Well, I am. Very, very busy. Good-bye."

She didn't back away. "But you're a cat.

 8

You're one of Bastet's own. We're supposed to protect the weak, remember? And there's a child here who needs our help."

"A child?" Khepri cut in. "Who?"

CHAPTER 2

Pampered

Miu looked startled. Evidently she hadn't noticed Khepri before. (A serious oversight, if you ask me. When you're a cat, observation is everything.)

"That's Khepri," I said.

"Pleased to meet you," Khepri said.

Miu bobbed her head at him. "Likewise."

After her rudeness to me, she was being friendly to a beetle? It made no sense. I closed my eyes, wishing she'd just go away.

But instead of leaving, she kept talking to Khepri. "The child's name is Tedimut. She works for Pharaoh's Great Wife, and she's been accused of stealing an amulet. But she didn't do it."

I opened one eye. "How do you know she didn't?"

"She wouldn't," Miu said. "She's the niece of my human, the cook Sebni, and I've known her since she was a baby. She's honest as can be, and she's very kindhearted. Before she started to serve the Great Wife, she worked in the kitchens, and she always did her best to look after us cats. Once, when I was a kitten, I got trapped in a storeroom, and she's the one who found me."

Khepri clicked in sympathy. "And now she's in trouble? Poor girl."

"No one knows what's become of her," Miu said. "Pharaoh's guards think she escaped the palace this morning, and they're searching the town. But I think maybe she's still here. I'm worried maybe the real thief hurt her, or tied her up somewhere." Miu turned to me. "I don't know these rooms. You do. You need to help me find her."

She wanted me to search through all the nooks and crannies of the palace for a child—a child who might not even be there? "I don't think so."

She meowed in protest. "But you're sworn to protect children—"

"I'm sworn to protect the children of my family," I said firmly. "That would be Pharaoh's family—his three sons and two daughters. They're all fine. The rest of the world is not my problem."

"I see." From underneath that torn ear of hers, Miu peered at me with disdain. "So it's true what they say—you really are a pampered nincompoop. You're too vain to lift so much as one paw for anyone else."

Nincompoop? Vain? I bristled at her, outraged.

"It isn't so much that he's vain," Khepri told her. "It's mostly that he's lazy."

"Khepri, whose side are you on?" I said. "No, don't answer that." I turned to Miu. "You can have a look around if you want to. I'm not stopping you. But leave me out of it. I don't waste time on things that aren't my problem." I turned away from her and started cleaning myself, to show her that the conversation was over.

Khepri gave me his most disapproving click. "Ra, you need to reconsider."

I shook my head.

"Never mind," Miu said behind us. "He's probably too slow and flabby to help me anyway. I'm better off going ahead on my own."

Well, that settled it. She wasn't getting any help from me.

Not that she was waiting for it. She was already halfway to the nearest doorway.

"No!" Khepri cried. "Not that way!"

His voice wasn't loud enough to carry far. Miu kept going.

Khepri turned to me. "Ra, you have to stop her."

"Maybe I'm too slow and flabby for that."

Khepri clicked his wings fiercely and jumped onto my head.

"Ouch!" I swatted at him, but scarab beetles are good at sticking tight.

Grabbing hold of the fur right next to my ear, Khepri whispered, "Ra, if you don't help her, do you know what I'll do? I'll stick dung in your snacks."

I sat bolt upright, my ears flattening in alarm. "You wouldn't!" I gasped. Dung in my snacks?

"Every day for a whole week," he chirped. "Your choice."

It wasn't much of one.

"All right," I said grudgingly. "Since you insist."

Let me make one point clear: I may lie around all day, but I'm not slow on my feet. When I want to run, I'm as fast as one of Pharaoh's chariots. Anyone in the palace will tell you that—especially any rat that dares to show its face. I intercepted Miu just before she reached the doorway.

"I wouldn't go in there if I were you," I said.

Miu tried to push past me. "I'm not listening to you anymore."

I blocked her. "You should. Keep going that way, and you'll land straight in front of Pharaoh's hunting dogs."

Miu leaped back. "Hunting dogs?"

"They're used to me, but they're deadly to strangers. Make the wrong move, and they'll eat you alive."

"Oh, dear." Miu's tail whipped around anxiously. "What am I going to do?"

"You're going to let us guide you around," Khepri said.

"What's this?" I hissed under my breath. "That wasn't part of our bargain."

"Oh, yes, it was," Khepri whispered, still holding on to the fur by my ear.

I tried to swat him off my head again and missed.

"I'd take you myself," Khepri explained to Miu, "but I don't know where everything is. I mostly stay outside, you see. There's more dung out here. But Ra knows everything about this palace. Don't you, Ra?"

"I might have forgotten," I said. "Being so pampered and all."

"Not just one week of dung," Khepri whispered in my ear. "Two."

"All right, all right," I said. "I'll show her around."

If it was the only way to save my snacks, I supposed I could take Miu through a couple of rooms. Maybe then Khepri would be reasonable. Even better, maybe Miu would decide to run ahead on her own.

The hold on my ear relaxed. "He's really a very decent creature at heart," Khepri said to Miu.

"A quick tour," I warned them. "That's all I'm promising."

"Fine with me," Miu said. "I'm in a hurry."

"Then let's get going." The sooner this was over, the better.

I led Miu across the courtyard to another, safer doorway. With Khepri still riding between my ears, we trotted into the palace.

CHAPTER 3

Beloved One

"Stay out of sight," I whispered to Miu as we slinked through the entranceway. "If the humans get a good look at you, they'll know you don't belong here. Not with that torn ear of yours."

Miu nodded and crouched even lower. I had to admit she was good at blending in. If you were a human you probably wouldn't even notice she was there. As we crept forward, I studied her, trying to figure out how she did it.

Maybe I studied a little too hard. I missed the footsteps coming our way.

"Ra, watch out!" Khepri warned. His legs tickled my fur as he slid down and hid under my belly.

DIRECTOR OF THE
ROYAL LOINCLOTHS

I looked up to see the Director of the Royal Loincloths closing in on me.

"Why, hello, Ra the Mighty. What on earth are you doing in here? Aren't they feeding you enough?" The Director's big laugh filled the passageway.

I stopped short, but there was no reason to worry. The Director was a good-natured man, and anyway, Miu was well hidden. Wasn't she? I glanced back to check.

My mistake.

"Oho!" The Director of the Royal Loincloths whistled. "Ra, you sly one, is that why you've come in to see us? You have a new friend? She is very charming," he added, peering down into the corner where Miu was pressed against the floor. "If a little ragged. Your sweetheart, yes?"

NO. *Absolutely not.* I stuck out my tongue to show what I thought of that idea.

Miu didn't seem to think much of it, either. She rolled her eyes at me and pretended to retch.

The Director of the Royal Loincloths looked worried. "Oh, dear. Your Beloved One isn't going to be sick, is she? The Overseer of the Royal Residence won't like that."

I was ready to retch myself. Beloved One?

Under my belly, I could feel Khepri giggling.

The Director of the Royal Loincloths shook his head. "You'd better take her back outside, Ra. I expect—" He broke off as someone called his name. "Coming, my lord!" Bending down to me, he whispered, "That's the Overseer. If you know what's good for you, you'll stay out of his way."

I was more than ready to take his advice. The Overseer pretended to like me in public, but he wasn't above prodding me with his foot when no one was around. If he saw Miu, he'd probably give each of us an outright kick.

I hurried down another passageway, one that connected Pharaoh's private quarters with the treasure room and the Great Wife's rooms.

"Hey, Miu's falling behind," Khepri whispered.

With a sigh, I turned back. Miu wasn't even looking our way. She was sniffing at the edge of a doorway that led toward another, wider passageway.

"Who's slow now?" I rounded back to her. "Miu, you need to keep up."

She touched her nose to the floor. "I think I've caught Tedimut's scent . . . no, it's gone. But she was somewhere around here, I'm sure." She started down the wider passageway.

"There's no point in going that way," I said.

Ignoring me, Miu streaked ahead, then came to a halt, staring at the chamber ahead of us.

I caught up with her. "You won't find the child here. There's nowhere to hide."

"So I see." She stared , her muzzle wavering as she took in the dazzling room. Even in the dim light, every surface gleamed— the polished columns, the smooth floors, the brilliant wall paintings of marshes and pools and gods. Farther back, a strong shaft of light illuminated a throne. "What *is* this place?"

"Pharaoh's audience hall." I hadn't wanted to play tour guide, but I was starting to enjoy it despite myself. I rarely had a chance to show off my royal domain. "This is where Pharaoh sits in state and receives his officials and visitors. There's a special spot reserved for me over there." I pointed my tail toward the little square under his throne.

How proud I'd been the first day I'd taken my place there! When the trumpets sounded, I was the one who led Pharaoh to the glittering seat of power. In the flaming light of the torches, all eyes were upon me. Even the Overseer had been forced to acknowledge my superiority.

Since then, there had been so many ceremonies that I was growing a little tired of them. Yet some parts of the job continued to give me a thrill. "I do love watching everyone bow down to us."

"Bow down to Pharaoh, you mean," said Khepri.

I shrugged. "It's all the same."

Khepri clicked his wings as if he thought that was funny, but it was only the truth.

Miu was still taking in the room. "The throne shines like cats' eyes."

"It's gilded with Nubian gold," I explained. "Only the best for Pharaoh."

"And for Pharaoh's Cat," murmured Khepri.

"Well, yes," I agreed. "I have my own gilded place in every single one of Pharaoh's throne rooms." I tilted my head toward Miu. As a kitchen cat, perhaps she didn't grasp what a sophisticated life I led. "He has a great many palaces, you know. This is my favorite, but I have to admit the one at Iunu is remarkable, too. And you really haven't lived till you've seen the throne room at Thebes. Though, to be honest, the most impressive thing about Thebes is the cook. He's devoted to me—brings me snacks every hour." I licked my whiskers just thinking about it. "Now that's what I call a palace."

"This palace would be better if it had more dung," Khepri said wistfully. "A nice big pile, right beside the throne."

I wrinkled my nose. "Dung? By the throne? You can't be serious, Khepri." Without waiting for an answer, I turned to more pleasant subjects. "Now, Miu, if you look at that wall painting behind the throne, you'll see something really splendid. Pharaoh himself insisted I sit for the portrait—"

To my annoyance, Miu turned away. "I'm not here to sightsee. I'm here to find Tedimut. And you're right: there's no way she could be hiding here. I'm going back to see if I can pick up her scent again."

"We'd all better go," Khepri warned. "Someone's coming!"

As we bounded back down the passageway, I heard the Overseer's crabby voice calling out to the Director of the Royal Loincloths. They were coming toward us. By the time we reached the place where Miu had picked up the child's scent, they were almost on our heels.

"Take cover," Khepri gasped.

With Khepri clinging fast to my fur, I headed for the only shelter I could see—a painted frieze that ran beneath the high, bright windows. From the ground, it looked like a long strip of lotus flowers, but I knew from my younger days that there was a ledge behind it where a cat could hide. Using a huge statue of Pharaoh as a ladder, I raced up to it, Miu close behind. We leaped onto the frieze and ducked down, just in time.

Below us, the Overseer and the Director of the Royal Loincloths walked past.

"I thought I saw that blasted cat up ahead of us," the Overseer said. "You saw him, too, didn't you?"

"No, my lord," the Director said quickly. "I wouldn't expect to find him here. He prefers to sit by the pool."

"In my experience, that cat is always where you least expect him to be." The Overseer stopped and looked behind him, as if searching for me. I was tempted to jump onto his head, but I restrained myself.

"You wouldn't believe how much trouble that cat can cause," the Overseer fretted. "It's all right for someone in your position, Director. You only have to see to the loincloths. But I have a whole palace to look after. I spent days—weeks!—making plans for the last royal banquet, and what does that cat do once the guests are in place? Start howling along with the court musicians."

"I was *singing*," I whispered indignantly to Miu. "I sounded great."

She gave me a warning look.

Below us, the Director chuckled. "I remember that, my lord. It was very amusing."

"Amusing?" The Overseer's voice was cold. "I think not. Nor was it amusing when he leaped onto the table and helped himself to the spiced ibex."

The Director's smile had vanished. "I'm sure he won't do that again, my lord."

"I should hope not." The Overseer started walking again. "If I ever catch that cat on a dinner table again, I'll let him have it. Why Pharaoh thinks so much of that animal is beyond me. All he does is eat—"

"Like he doesn't eat plenty himself," I muttered to Khepri. "He's sore because I took a bit of liver from his plate. He needs to get better about sharing."

"Shhh!" Miu said.

After that, we kept still until the humans were gone.

"Whew!" Khepri said. "That was close. It's a good thing you knew where to hide, Ra."

I waited for Miu to thank me, too, but she was sniffing at the brickwork.

A moment later, her tail went up like a flag, and she mewed in excitement. "Tedimut was here!"

"Behind this frieze?" I gave her a doubtful glance. "Humans are so clumsy, and they're no good with heights. How would she have gotten up here?"

"Tedimut could do it," Miu said confidently. "Maybe she used that big statue to get up here, the way we did. She's small, but a good climber. The day she rescued me, I was caught on the top shelf in the storeroom, way at the back. She climbed up high and squeezed behind jars and crates to find me, almost as if she were a cat herself. And after she freed me, she had to do it all backward, with me in her arms. So this would be easy for her." Still sniffing, she moved along the frieze. "Yes, no question about it. Tedimut was definitely here."

Miu took her time checking out the brickwork, then stopped short under one of the high windows. "Oh, dear. I've lost her again." She went a bit farther down the frieze, then came back. "Yes, this is where the trail ends."

If there is *a trail*, I thought. "How about we move along with the tour, then? I'd like to be back at the pool by snack time."

Miu ignored me. So did Khepri. They were both looking up at the window.

"Do you think she went out that way?" Khepri asked.

"Oh, come on," I said before Miu could answer. "You can't tell me a child could leap all the way up there—"

Before I could say anything more, Miu sprang up the wall toward the window. I thought she would fall, but she made it to the sill. Again her nose went down. "Yes, this is where she went," she called back to us. "I can smell her."

Miu leaped out the window and disappeared.

CHAPTER 4

Across the Roof

"What are you waiting for, Ra?" Khepri said after Miu vanished. "Follow her!"

I sat where I was and gave my face a little wash. "She seems to be fine on her own," I said. "And it's getting awfully close to snack time. I think it's best if I go back to the pool."

Khepri groaned. "Ra! How can you think about snacks right now? Don't you want to find the child?"

"Not if it means missing snacks," I said honestly.

Khepri sighed. "Ra, it's not nearly as late as you think it is. It's going to be a while till your next snack, and there's plenty of time to find the child first."

I considered this. Khepri was a better timekeeper than I was, and he was usually right about the snack schedule. Still, I hesitated.

"But maybe leaping up onto that windowsill is a bit too much for you," Khepri said. "Miu could do it, of course, but she's stronger and fitter—"

"She is *not!* I can do it, too. With my eyes closed." I took a running leap at the wall. "Watch me!"

All right, so eyes closed wasn't the best strategy. Even with my eyes open, it took three tries to get up to the windowsill.

"I don't care what that cat thinks she can smell," I grumbled to Khepri, who'd burrowed down into my neck fur. "There is no way a child could do this."

"I suppose she must have a good sense of balance," Khepri said.

"Better than Pharaoh's Cat? A human?" I sniffed. "I doubt it."

Outside the window there was a series of roofs. When I jumped onto the first one, I saw Miu on the next level up, with her nose to the tiles. It looked like she'd picked up some sort of scent.

Khepri said in a worried voice, "I do hope Miu knows what she's doing."

"You and me both," I said. "This is all starting to feel like a wild-goose chase."

Before we could get anywhere near Miu, she was off and running onto yet another adjoining roof.

"Make that a wild-*ostrich* chase," I grumbled to Khepri. "Where did that cat learn to run so fast?"

Above me Khepri chuckled. "I guess kitchen cats don't spend all their time lying by the pool."

"Their loss," I said. "I tell you, I'm ready to go back to the pool right now." Which was true. But it was also true that being up here on the roof was reminding me of my younger, more adventurous days, before I became Pharaoh's Cat. I felt the stirrings of curiosity. Had Miu really found a trail up here? And if so, where did it lead?

By the time I caught up with Miu, my curiosity was stretching thin. We'd practically crisscrossed the entire palace, and I was sure I was about to expire of heatstroke. But did anyone praise me for the efforts I was making? No.

"What took you so long?" Miu said as we came up to her. "I thought you'd never catch up. Here, have a look at this." She showed us a small vent in the brickwork that ran underneath another connecting roof. "See how a corner of this wooden grate is broken off? This is the way Tedimut went. I can tell from the smell."

Hopping off me, Khepri held on tight to the grate with his legs and poked his head through one of the holes. "I think you're right," he said, turning back to Miu. "It's very dark in there, but it looks like a storeroom to me. That would be a good place to hide."

I was still staring at the window. It was high time I brought some common sense to the proceedings. "Miu, the hole in that grate isn't even big enough for a cat. What makes you think a human could get through it?"

"A human could pry the grate out," Khepri suggested. "And then bang it back into place. Maybe that's why there's a hole in it."

"That's what I was thinking," Miu said eagerly. "The question is, can we follow her? Khepri, you can, for sure—"

"Not by myself," Khepri said. "A cat could manage the drop, or a human, but not a beetle. I'd never get back up again. We need to get you two through the vent, too."

Miu started to pace with anxiety. "But how?"

She and Khepri studied the vent.

"You know, we might just be able to pull the whole grate out, the way Tedimut did," Khepri said slowly. "If you look at it, you can see it's a little loose in places. Ra, maybe you could grab the broken end of that bit of wood with your teeth?"

He wanted Pharaoh's Cat to gnaw on broken wood? And end up with a tongue full of splinters? I glared at Khepri, outraged. "I don't think so."

Miu slid past me. "I'll do it."

"Okay," Khepri said as she positioned herself. "Now bite down and pull back as hard as you can."

Miu jerked back, but the grate didn't budge.

"We need more power," Khepri said.

There was a long pause while they both looked back at me.

"Oh, all right," I said. "But if I get splinters, Khepri, you're the one picking them out." I lined myself up next to Miu and bit down on the wood.

"One, two three, PULL!" Khepri shouted.

We pulled. The grate shifted. When I sank my teeth in deeper and yanked, it popped out.

"Ouch!"

As I spat out a mouthful of splinters, Miu shot through the vent. Once my mouth was free of wood chips—I made Khepri inspect it—I poked my head through. It was too dark to see anything.

"You know what, Khepri?" I said. "I think it's time to head back."

"The only way back is across that sweltering roof," Khepri said. "And I thought you were dying of heat."

He had a point. The air from the vent was nice and cool. "All right," I said. "We'll go inside for a little bit, but then we go back. Our part of the job is done. Everything else is up to Miu."

I hopped through the vent, Khepri riding on my head, and landed on the edge of a slatted shelf. It took a moment for my eyes to adjust, but then I saw the space clearly. Khepri was right: it was a storeroom, stacked with shelves of clay jars, the kind that usually stored oil. I rubbed my ears against their cool, smooth sides. It made a nice change from the sun on the roof.

"Hey, watch out!" Khepri scuttled down my neck. "You nearly knocked me off there, Ra."

"Don't tempt me," I said, but I stepped back from the jars. When Khepri keeps still—and quiet—it's easy to forget that he's on my head.

Below us Miu cried out. "Tedimut!"

Khepri jumped down onto the slats. "She found the girl! Where are they? I can't see them."

"Neither can I. Hold on." I had to admit I was interested in seeing this girl who could climb like a cat. I lowered my head and motioned for Khepri to join me, and we peered through a gap in the slats. On the next shelf down, between the wall and the tall jars, crouched a young girl. I'm not good at estimating human ages, but I'd say she was no more than ten or eleven years old—about the age of the Pharaoh's oldest son.

Not that this child was one of Pharaoh's, I reminded myself. She was a servant. Which meant she was not my responsibility. Still, my whiskers were quivering with curiosity again. How had she ended up here?

As we watched, Miu jumped into Tedimut's lap.

"Oh, Miu! However did you find me?" The girl's whisper was barely louder than breathing.

We heard the rumble of Miu's answering purr.

I picked my way through the clay jars until I had a better view of the shelf below. Miu was up to something with that purr, and I didn't want to miss what happened next.

CHAPTER 5

Cat Magic

Some people believe cats are magic, and who am I to disagree? But when people say cats can *work* magic . . . well, that's a little more complicated. Certainly the old stories tell of the great sun god Ra, my ancestor, turning into a cat to defend our land from the forces of chaos. His daughter, the great cat goddess Bastet, is worshipped to this day for holding evil spirits and disease at bay.

But I'll tell you a secret (and may the curse of Bastet be upon you if you tell anyone else): I've never met a cat who had that kind of power. Including me. Our magic is this: if we purr in *just* the right way, we can usually make you humans talk.

How it works, I really don't know. It's a

magic that's strongest with our own families, the humans we are sworn to protect, though sometimes we can get strangers to talk, too. The purr has to be a full-body purr, and it helps if we sit on your lap or twine around your legs or turn belly-up.

To be honest, I find the whole process undignified. I rarely attempt it, even with family.

Miu, however, had no such reservations. She was sprawled across Tedimut's lap like a fur piece. And since Tedimut was the niece of Miu's cook, and therefore part of Miu's family, her purr was doubly powerful. It didn't surprise me at all when Tedimut started to talk.

"I didn't do it," Tedimut whispered to Miu. "I didn't take it. No matter what they say, I didn't."

Ho-hum, I thought. *She would say that, wouldn't she?* But I kept my ears up, listening. There was something about the girl that reminded me of my favorite of Pharaoh's daughters, the one who always treats me with the respect I deserve. Maybe it was her soft, sure voice. Or maybe it was the delicate way she stroked Miu.

The girl had an almost catlike grace about her. I wanted to hear her side of the story.

"I didn't even want to touch it," Tedimut whispered. "That amulet is worth a fortune, and for a servant like me that means trouble. If you drop it, or even hold it the wrong way, you can be punished. But Lady Shepenupet said I had to take it back to the treasure room. She was very angry. She said the Great Wife didn't care for the amulet, and it should never have been brought to the robing room. She wanted me to return it before everyone woke and the Great Wife discovered the mistake."

Lady Shepenupet? I wasn't a fan. She was the tall, peevish woman who was always at the Great Wife's side. Last year she'd complained about my getting cat hair on the Great Wife's ceremonial tunic. I saw that tunic up close, and let me tell you, cat hair improved it. But you'd never know it from the way Lady Shepenupet carried on.

Plus, the lady is sneaky. When she showed the tunic to the Great Wife, the Great Wife laughed and fed me antelope chunks, so Lady Shepenupet forced a laugh, too. But that night there was a strange-smelling bit of meat on my snack tray. Coincidence? Maybe. But I didn't go near it.

I moved a bit closer to Tedimut.

"I think it must have been Lady Shepenupet herself who made the mistake," the girl said softly. "She's the one who orders the Great Wife's jewels from the treasure room and sets them out every day. But I'm the youngest of the Great Wife's servants, so Lady Shepenupet blames me for everything. And I can't complain, or I'll lose my position. So I did as Lady Shepenupet asked,

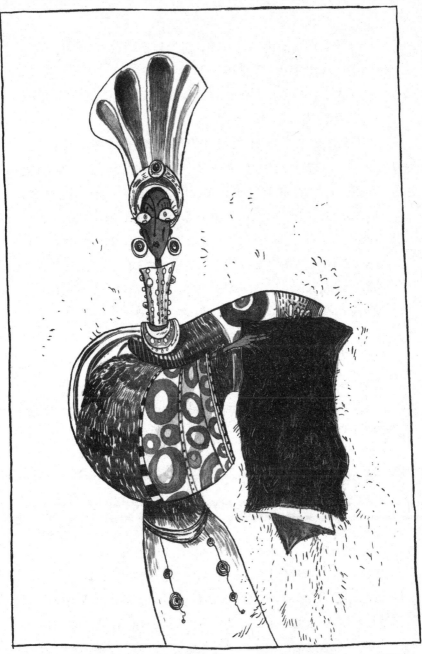

LADY SHEPENUPET

and I took the amulet back to the treasure room. Or I tried to, at least . . ."

As Tedimut faltered, Miu purred as loudly as an army of locusts.

Hugging her close, Tedimut went on. "It was just before dawn, and hardly anyone was around. I ran as fast as I could, but I don't know that part of the palace very well, and I lost my way. I stopped to get my bearings, and something came flying at my head. I think maybe it was a stone. When I came to, the amulet was gone."

She buried herself in Miu's fur.

"Look at that bump," Khepri murmured in my ear. "*Something* sure hit her."

I nodded. In the shaft of light from the vent, you could see a lump the size of a duck's egg on the side of Tedimut's head. I winced. That had to hurt.

"I was so scared, Miu," Tedimut whispered. "I thought at first I'd only dropped the amulet, but it was nowhere to be seen. Then I heard Lady Shepenupet shouting my name. I knew she would blame me for losing the amulet. I would be beaten, and if she accused me of stealing it, they might even cut off my nose. So I climbed up to the window—"

"The window where Miu found her scent," Khepri whispered.

"—and I escaped," Tedimut finished. "I crossed the roof like a cat, Miu, and I found this hiding place."

Clever, agile, resourceful . . . this girl really *was* like a cat. I was impressed.

"But what do I do now? I can't stay here forever. I'm already so thirsty and hungry. And there's nothing here for me to eat or drink—only jars and jars of olive oil." Tedimut gulped. "But if I try to leave, I'll be caught, and then it's all over."

She was stuck here with no snacks? Poor girl! But I agreed that she had to stay put. "She's right," I said to Khepri. "There are guards all over the palace, and they'll be watching for her."

Overhearing, Miu lifted her head and looked up at me. "That's not the only problem. That Pharaoh of yours has offered a reward for Tedimut's capture, so everyone else will be looking for her, too."

"He's not just my pharaoh," I said, stung.

"He's yours, too." *Even if he has made a mistake this time*, I added silently. I would never be disloyal enough to say so aloud, but—between you and me—Pharaoh does slip up occasionally. By now I was pretty sure that this was one of those times.

"You're Pharaoh's Cat," Miu said to me. "You need to make him see reason."

"You want *Ra* to reason with Pharaoh?" Khepri gave an incredulous click. "He doesn't have that kind of power, Miu. I mean, when all's said and done, he's just a cat."

"*Just* a cat?" Miu and I chorused indignantly, at exactly the same time.

"Well, you know what I mean," said Khepri.

"No, I don't," Miu said, and for the first time I agreed with her.

"What is it, Miu?" Tedimut craned her head upward, trying to see what Miu was meowing about. "Is there something up there?"

I darted back, trying to stay out of sight, only to find that Khepri was in my way. Pharaoh's Cat is a model of grace, of course, but a slippery beetle is a challenge even for me. Paws grappling for balance, I tried to save myself from falling through the slats.

"Ra!" Khepri lunged for my tail.

That did it. Twisting and clawing at the air, I toppled with Khepri to the shelf below. I landed right in front of Tedimut, in an awkward half-crouch.

Tedimut stared at me in astonishment. Curled in her lap, Miu blinked in disbelief.

It was not my best moment, but it got even worse. Before I could pull myself together, the door to the storeroom creaked open.

My ears swiveled. I couldn't see the door. The clay jars were in the way. But I knew what that sound meant.

A guard, I thought. *Hunting down Tedimut.*

The door opened wider, and the gloom of the storeroom brightened. Tedimut bit her lower lip, but otherwise she stayed as motionless as a column in Pharaoh's audience hall.

Honestly, a cat couldn't have done it better.

Sandals pattered across the floor. I tensed. So did Tedimut.

"What are you doing?" someone shouted from the door. "You've got the wrong storeroom. Those jars are full of oil. Try the next storeroom down—and be quick about it."

The sandals scuffed their way out. The door banged shut.

Tedimut heaved a shaky sigh.

That was close, I thought.

To my surprise, my heart was racing faster than it had in years. Determined to regain my usual poise, I snapped out of my awkward crouch and arranged myself in the time-honored Bastet pose: chin up, front paws extended, eyes narrowed, ears alert. My slender collar gleamed in the dim light from the vent.

Of course, Khepri was still sticking fast to my tail, but I did my best to ignore that. Symmetry and perfection, that's what I was after. Classic elegance.

Tedimut watched me.

"Are you . . . *Pharaoh's Cat*?" she whispered. Even in the shadows, her eyes shone. She glanced down at Miu, still in her lap. "Oh, Miu, you brought him to save me, didn't you? Thank you, thank you." To me,

she bowed
her head.
"O Great
One, Defender
of the Small, Lord
of the Powerful Paw,
I entrust myself to
your care."

Khepri fluttered
his wings. "Honestly.
The way people treat
you, Ra . . ."

"I don't see what's so
wrong," I said.

Khepri hopped off my tail.
"What's wrong, my dear Ra, is that now
she expects you to save her."

"Well, yes, I did gather that." Khepri
always thinks he's so much smarter than
me. But this time I was one step ahead of
him. I puffed up my chest. "Saving her is
exactly what I'm going to do."

Miu and Khepri both froze.

"You're going to save her?" Khepri
repeated in disbelief. "*You?*"

Miu looked like she'd swallowed her

dinner the wrong way. "How can you possibly help, Ra?"

"Why, by taking the case," I said grandly. "Miu, you look after the child. Khepri, you stay with them. I'm off to solve this crime."

CHAPTER 6

On the Hunt

Miu and Khepri stared at me openmouthed. I could tell I had impressed them. I trotted forward and nuzzled Tedimut's bowed head in my best regal manner. "Never fear, child. You're in the paws of Pharaoh's Cat now."

The child didn't understand me, of course. But when she raised her head, the awe in her bright eyes was gratifying.

I nodded graciously at her and turned to go.

"Wait!" Khepri latched onto my tail, trying to pin me down. "What do you think you're doing, Ra? Cats don't solve mysteries."

"It's not such a bad idea," Miu said thoughtfully to Khepri. "If we can find out who the true thief is, then we have a chance of saving Tedimut. And a cat like Ra can go wherever he wants in the palace. He could find out clues for us." In a more doubtful voice, she added, "Although whether he could make any sense of those clues is another question."

"You forget who I am," I said proudly. "I'm Pharaoh's Cat—Ra the Mighty. I can do anything I like." I pulled free of Khepri and climbed toward the tiny vent where we'd entered.

"Wait!" Khepri called out. "You're going to need help. Take me with you."

"Oh, no." I was nearly at the vent. "This is a mission for Pharaoh's Cat, and Pharaoh's Cat alone."

"But you have to take me," Khepri said. "Otherwise I'll put—"

"Dung in my snacks?" I didn't turn around. "Don't even think about it, Khepri. A bargain is a bargain, and I did what you wanted. If you go back on your terms, you'll have the gods to deal with."

Khepri was quiet, but Miu stirred from her place beside Tedimut. "But surely you need a sidekick, Ra," she purred up to me.

I stopped in midstride. "A what?"

"A sidekick. An assistant. All great detectives have one," she explained.

I ran a paw over my whiskers. "They do?"

Khepri scrambled up toward me. "Yes, Ra. It's one of the rules."

I nodded, trying to make it look as if I'd always known that.

"Okay," I said as Khepri hopped onto my tail. "You can come with me. But remember how it works: *you're* the sidekick, and *I'm* the Great Detective."

"That's right, Khepri," Miu said.

I thought I saw her wink. But maybe it was just the light.

"Oh, you'll be the one leading us," Khepri promised me as he climbed onto my back. "I'll just be there in the background, getting baffled, and asking you to explain things to me, and being amazed by your powers of deduction. You know—a sidekick."

I nodded again. Really, what a perfect role for Khepri. In my experience, beetles are good at keeping to the background.

"Then off we go," I said. With Khepri clinging tight to my head, I jumped through the vent.

At first it was a relief to be back in the light, but as soon as I began trotting across the baking roof, my paws started to hurt.

"So where are we going?" Khepri asked.

I wasn't quite sure, but I didn't plan to tell him that. I glanced around, trying to orient myself, though all I could really think about was my poor scorched paws.

Khepri was looking around, too. "I think we're near the Great Wife's quarters."

My paws had suffered enough. "And that's exactly where we're headed," I said, jumping through the nearest window.

Up on my head, Khepri gave an approving click. "Good choice, Ra. If you ask me, the best place to start is the Great Wife's robing room—"

"I don't believe I did ask you, Khepri."

"Er . . . right," Khepri said. "You had another idea, then?"

I did—and it wasn't the robing room. Instead I headed straight for the doors I'd seen, which led into the Great Wife's bedroom. As I expected, the guards let me through. They hadn't seen me here in some time, but Pharaoh's Cat may walk where he likes. And even if he has a beetle on his head, nobody makes a fuss.

As we went in, Lady Nefrubity came hurrying out. She didn't pay any attention to me. She never does. But then I don't pay much attention to her, either. She used to serve Pharaoh's mother, and she wears more black kohl on her eyes than anyone else in the palace, but in all the time I've known her, I've never heard her say anything interesting, or talk above a mumble. And she's certainly never offered me any treats.

I stalked right past her.

"Wow." As we came through the doorway, Khepri shuffled higher on my head to get a better view. "This is some room."

"This is nothing," I said. "You should see Pharaoh's room. It's twice the size." Still, this one had its charms. Light and airy, it had a huge bed and windows that opened onto a garden. It was full of good memories, too. From time to time, I visited the Great Wife, and she would feed me tidbits from her snack plates.

Some people say the Great Wife has a temper, but I've never seen it. She adores animals, and she's always very generous. At least she is with her favorites—like me. And she loves snacks almost as much as I do.

"This place looks pretty fancy to me. Gilded bed, gilded chairs, painted walls . . ." Khepri was straining so hard to see everything that he nearly toppled over onto my nose. "No dung, though," he finished sadly.

"Right," I said. "Because that's just what every Great Wife wants in her bedroom. Dung."

"Yes," Khepri agreed. "When I marry, I'll bring my wife fresh dung balls every day."

"Don't invite me to the wedding, Khepri." I looked around. Dung wasn't the only thing missing from this room. The Great Wife wasn't here, and neither were her ladies.

"They must have gone out," I said, disappointed. Now that I thought about it, I did remember hearing something earlier this morning about Pharaoh and the Great Wife attending ceremonies in the temple today. Which meant there wouldn't be any special treats for me from the Great Wife's plate . . .

. . . unless there were leftovers somewhere.

I sniffed the air. It smelled like there was spiced meat on the other side of the bed. Hoping for the best, I rounded the corner and stopped short.

I'd nearly stumbled over Aat, the Great Wife's leopard.

Aat was sleeping, of course. She sleeps even more than I do—and when she isn't sleeping, she's grooming herself. Like the Great Wife, she prides herself on looking beautiful. And I suppose Aat *is* sort of beautiful, if you like your beauty with a side order of ferocious teeth and claws.

Khepri obviously didn't. "Yikes!"

"Hold on," I whispered as he scuttled back toward my neck. The light from the windows was shining on a plate on the floor—and the plate had chunks of goat on it. All I had to do was tiptoe around Aat, and that meat would be mine.

I was a whisker's length from the plate when Khepri lost his grip and hit the floor. *Click!*

He wasn't hurt, but the sound woke up Aat. "Intruders!" Her eyes only half open, she trapped us between her claws.

CHAPTER 7

What Aat Saw

Aat's claws scraped dangerously close to my tail.

"Stop that!" I yelped as Khepri ducked for cover under my belly. "Aat, it's me. Pharaoh's Cat."

"Oh." Aat withdrew her claws a smidgen. Her yellow eyes glared at me above her heavy gold collar. Studded with jewels, it matched one that the Great Wife sometimes wore—except that Aat's collar was attached to a long golden chain. Although Aat didn't like to talk about it, the other end of the chain was tied around a stone pillar. "What are you doing here, Fluffball?"

"She calls you *Fluffball*?" Khepri said in a tiny voice.

Aat

It's true. Aat's called me that for years, probably because she knows I hate it. What kind of name is *Fluffball* for a cat of consequence? You'd think Aat would show some respect now that I'm Pharaoh's Cat. After all, my human is the Pharaoh; I outrank her. But it was no use giving Aat a lecture on manners, especially not when her claws were so close.

"Why is that little beetle burrowing into your fur?" Aat wrinkled her enormous nose. "You're not wearing him as an accessory, are you? It's not a good look for you, Fluffball."

"Khepri's my friend."

Aat made a face. "So what brings you and your little *friend* here? Let me guess: you're looking for snacks." She glanced at the plate. "I hope you weren't thinking of eating that goat meat, Fluffball. The Great Wife left it there for me."

It wasn't a good idea to show interest in any food that Aat wanted. "Goat? I hadn't noticed."

"You, not notice food?" Aat's mouth rippled in a toothy smile. "How very funny, Fluffball. What else would bring you here?"

"Investigations!" hissed Khepri from under my fur.

He was right. I'd almost forgotten. "Actually, Aat, I came to talk to you about jewelry."

I figured that would get her attention. Aat loves jewelry even more than the Great Wife does, and that's saying something.

Aat looked me over, twirling her spotted tail. "I can see why you'd want advice, Fluffball. If you ask me, you should get yourself a proper scarab. One made of stone. Live beetles are just too, too disgusting."

"Khepri's not disgusting," I said. "Scarab beetles are very neat by nature." *As long as you ignore the way they like to play around with dung.* "Anyway, that's not what I wanted to ask about."

Aat was losing interest in the conversation. Watching her tail more than me, she asked, "Then why are you here?"

"Because I heard the Great Wife lost a valuable amulet this morning," I told her. "Do you know anything about it?"

"I should say so!" Aat forgot her tail and sat up straight, eyes gleaming. "I saw everything. And that little thief completely *ruined* my morning grooming session."

An eyewitness! I hadn't expected that, given that Aat was usually chained up. "So you know who the thief was?"

"Of course. It was that stupid little servant girl, the newest one. I can't remember her name. Starts with a *T* . . ."

Uh-oh. Had I made a big mistake in trusting that bright-eyed girl? I didn't want to believe it was possible. "You mean Tedimut? You saw her steal the amulet?"

"Yes, that's the name." Aat's eyes were still blazing with anger. "And of course I didn't see it, Fluffball. How could I? I was right here where I was supposed to be, on my sleeping cushion, waiting for her to groom me." She glanced back at the cushion, which was near the door of the bedroom. "That's one of her duties every morning—to look after me. And she never came. I was wondering where she was when Lady Shepenupet started shouting her name. Everyone went hunting for her, and when they came back, they said she'd stolen the amulet."

"But no one actually saw her take it?" I asked, just to be sure.

"We didn't need to," Aat growled. "The amulet is missing, and so is she. Isn't that proof enough?"

I hadn't been a fool to trust Tedimut after all.

"Besides," Aat went on, "it's not the first time things have disappeared. Ever since that girl started working here, we've had problems. Lady Shepenupet should have dismissed her weeks ago."

"What sorts of things have gone missing?" I asked.

"Little trinkets," said Aat. "A strand of beads. An ivory comb. The girl was lucky that the Great Wife was fond of her, and that she *wasn't* fond of what went missing. In the end, the Great Wife decided she must have misplaced the things herself. But the girl went one step too far when she took that amulet. This time she'll be punished."

"But you don't have proof that Tedimut took those other things?" I asked Aat.

"I don't need proof," Aat said airily. "Leopards are very sensitive. We can detect a guilty conscience at fifty paces. I know it's that girl who stole the Eye of Horus amulet."

So it was an Eye of Horus amulet that had gone missing? Interesting.

If you ever visit the palace, you'll see the Eye of Horus everywhere, in wall paintings and on furniture and, yes, on amulets, too. These amulets are made in all sorts of colors and sizes, but what they have in common is the shape: the curving lines of the eye of the great falcon god Horus. The symbol offers health and protection, particularly to Pharaoh but to others, too.

Still buried in my belly fur, Khepri whispered, "Ask her exactly what this amulet looks like."

Aat regarded Khepri with disgusted fascination. "Ooooh, that beetle thing of yours . . . it said something."

"It was just a sneeze." I didn't want her to think I was taking orders from Khepri, but he had a point. It would be useful to know more about the missing amulet. "What makes this Eye of Horus so valuable, Aat? Is it covered with jewels?"

Aat yawned. "I really can't remember. It

used to belong to Pharaoh's mother, and all her stuff is so clunky. Not the Great Wife's style at all. The Great Wife wore the Eye once or twice when Pharaoh gave it to her, but I think she only did it to please him."

So the Great Wife wanted to keep on the right side of Pharaoh? Fair enough. As did everyone else in Egypt.

"I'm not surprised she had Lady Shepenupet put it away," Aat continued. "The Great Wife was never one of the Royal Mother's favorites, so why should she wear her old jewelry? Even if it was pretty—which it isn't—the Great Wife would rather wear her own adornments. You've seen her gold-and-amethyst necklace, haven't you? Too marvelous for words." Aat licked her lips. "To tell the truth, I think the Great Wife is glad that old amulet is gone. It's Pharaoh who's furious."

"With her?" I asked.

"Of course not!" Aat rolled her eyes as if I'd said something stupid. "Pharaoh adores the Great Wife. Everyone knows that. He's furious with the *thief*."

I mulled this over. Pharaoh certainly did

⁓THE GREAT WIFE⁓

adore his wife, just as she adored him, and they hated to argue with each other. Yet they both liked getting their own way. It was a complicated relationship.

"It's so awkward, having an accessory that doesn't suit you," Aat went on. "Almost anything is justified."

"Ask her who was here this morning," Khepri hissed, poking his head out of my belly fur again.

Head tilted, Aat stared at him. "Is that thing *talking* to you, Fluffball?"

"Another sneeze," I said. If Khepri thought I was going to ask such a silly question, he could think again. Who cared who was in the Great Wife's room this morning? After all, the amulet wasn't stolen from here. It was stolen from Tedimut while she was lost in the palace.

Khepri wriggled with impatience against my belly. "*Ask her.*"

"Another sneeze," I told Aat, trying not to laugh. Khepri's legs were tickling me.

Aat gave us a cold stare. "I don't like all these sneezes, Fluffball. That thing better not make me sick."

"It's something only beetles get," I assured her. "Not leopards."

Khepri was wriggling worse than ever. To make him stop, I gave in and asked his question. "Aat, who was in the Great Wife's room this morning? Was there anyone missing? Or anyone extra?"

"Everything was as usual," Aat said. "Well, until Lady Shepenupet started shouting, and the girl didn't come, and everyone rushed out hunting for her."

"Everyone?" I repeated.

"Well, everyone who counts."

"Who exactly was in the room?" I was growing impatient but tried not to show it. "Before they started hunting for the girl, I mean."

"Oh, they were all in their usual places," Aat said. "Lady Shepenupet spent most of her time scolding the younger servants, of course. She never lets them get away with anything, and quite right, too. Someone has to keep them in line, and it certainly won't be Lady Nefrubity. She's supposed to look after the Great Wife's sandals and sashes, but all she ever does is talk about her family. The way that woman goes on about her nieces and nephews! You'd think they were royalty themselves, but they most certainly are not."

"No," I agreed. I'd heard the family was down on its luck and struggling to keep up whatever status they had. "So Lady Shepenupet and Lady Nefrubity were there. And who else?"

"Lady Tawerettenru and Lady Wedjebten were chattering away and laying out the Great Wife's tunic and sash, as they always do. Suddenly Lady Shepenupet started shouting, and she and the other ladies rushed out, screaming the girl's name. The Great Wife and I were left alone to cope with just five servants—the youngest ones. Not a single one of them thought about me and how much my coat needed brushing. They all rushed around serving the Great Wife." Aat sniffed. "I had to wait until noon before I was properly groomed."

"What a tragedy," Khepri said, a touch too loudly.

"That wasn't a sneeze." Aat glared at Khepri. "That thing is talking, Fluffball. And it sounds like it's making fun of me."

"You misheard him," I said quickly. "It was a compliment. He was, er . . . admiring your collar."

"Oh." Aat threw Khepri a suspicious look, but when he stayed quiet she curved her neck proudly so that the golden collar sparkled and the jewels caught the light. "Well, he ought to admire it. Everyone should. It's the most gorgeous collar in the palace." She glanced at my own slender strand of gold. "Much nicer than yours, Fluffball. And much more expensive. Pharaoh doesn't seem to think you're worth much, does he?"

"Don't be ridiculous," I said. "Pharaoh would cover me in jewels if that were what I wanted. But he knows I prefer a light collar—one that doesn't come with a chain."

It's true: I really don't like being tied down by bejeweled trappings. But mentioning the chain was a bad idea. Aat growled again and took a swipe at me. I leaped out of reach, but she followed me, stalking me across the floor.

"Get out of here, Fluffball," she snarled. "Go back to your pool. This is *my* room, and you're wasting my time."

I don't know if you've ever met an angry leopard, but my advice is not to argue. "I'm going, I'm going."

"Wait." Khepri scrambled up my side. "I have one more question."

He never got to ask it. As he spoke, Aat lunged—and I ran.

CHAPTER 8

Bringing up Bebi

I didn't stop running till we were outside the Great Wife's bedroom, well out of Aat's reach.

"That went well," I said to Khepri, once I had my breath back.

"You mean we came out alive?" Khepri croaked from behind my neck. "To be honest, Ra, I was hoping for something a little better than that."

"Don't be such a wet blanket," I said. "I tell you, I've just about cracked this case."

"You have?" Khepri slid off my back and came around to face me, looking surprised. "What do you mean?"

"It's quite simple, really." I licked my paw. "Thanks to Aat, we know that the amulet isn't the only thing that's gone missing. There's that string of beads, and the comb, too. All we have to do is find them, and ta-dah! We'll have our thief."

"How can you be sure the same thief took all of them?" Khepri wanted to know. "And how are you going to find the beads and comb when you don't know what they look like?"

"Details," I said. "Petty details."

"*Important* details," Khepri insisted. "Do you realize we nearly lost our lives to that leopard, and we still don't really know what that Eye of Horus amulet looks like?"

"Sure we do," I said. "*Clunky.*"

Khepri sighed. "That could describe half the jewelry in this palace, Ra. It's not enough to identify anything."

"Well, it's just a wild guess, but I bet it looks like an eye," I said. "That should narrow it down."

"Not really," Khepri said. "We don't know if it's the size of a date or a dinner plate, or whether it's made of gold or copper or silver, or if it has jewels in it. That's what I wanted to ask Aat: Does she know someone who can tell us more? Because without a good description, I don't see how we'll ever find the amulet—or the thief."

Maybe it was true that we could use a better description of the amulet. But it was also true that Khepri sometimes finds it hard to look on the bright side. If you ask me, it comes of spending too much time with dung.

"Trust me," I said. "We're on the right track. There's no mystery so deep that Pharaoh's Cat can't get to the bottom of it. You're just feeling discouraged, that's all."

"Right," said Khepri, but he didn't sound comforted.

"Besides," I went on, "I already know someone who can tell us more about the amulet."

Khepri perked up. "You do?"

I nodded. "Aat said the amulet used to belong to Pharaoh's mother. So that means Bebi should know all about it. He never forgets anything." Even better, Bebi was good about sharing food. At last I might get that snack I was longing for.

Khepri looked uneasy. "Is Bebi the old

baboon that belongs to Pharaoh's mother?"

"Yes, he's been with her since he was a baby—a very long time ago. Haven't you met before?"

"Er ... no. Dung beetles don't make a habit of introducing themselves to baboons."

"Why not?" I asked.

"Because they eat our young, that's why!" Khepri waved his forelegs in the air. "At a pinch, they might even try to eat *us*."

"Bebi would never be so rude as to do that." I chuckled at the very idea. "He was a friend of my father's, and he's quite a cultured fellow. You'll see."

"Maybe you should do this interview without me," Khepri said.

There was a pause while we both considered this.

Not a bad idea, I thought. I could do without Khepri hiding in my fur and hissing questions at me, the way he did with Aat.

"No problem," I said. "It's not like I can't handle this investigation by myself."

But Khepri was already shaking his head. "I don't know what I was thinking, Ra." He took a flying leap into my fur. "Forget it. I'm coming with you!"

"I'm having second thoughts," Khepri whispered as we reached Pharaoh's mother's rooms.

"It's a little late now," I told him as the guards let us through. "There's Bebi."

The old baboon ambled toward us, his thick puffs of silver hair gleaming in the soft light. They surrounded his bare snout, forming a hood and cape that made him look twice as big as he really was.

Like Aat, he wore a bejeweled golden collar, but in Bebi's case there was no chain attached. All baboons were strong, and some were violent, but Bebi had long since proved himself to be the most peaceable of souls. I didn't visit him often, but when I did, I always found him good company.

"You're sure he won't try to eat me?" Khepri whispered.

"Shhhh!" I said. And just in time, too, because we'd reached Bebi, who was holding out his hands in welcome.

Bebi

"Ra the Mighty! Great Pharaoh's Cat! It's been too long." Bowing low, Bebi touched his hand to my head in greeting. He knew what was due to me as Pharaoh's Cat, and it was like him to observe all the courtesies. But his polite gesture sent Khepri scuttling down my back, searching for cover.

"Ah!" Bebi drew back. "My dear Ra, did you know that you have a passenger?"

"He's a friend," I said. "Bebi, meet Khepri. Khepri, meet Bebi."

Bebi bent his head down to Khepri. "A pleasure."

Khepri mumbled something that I couldn't quite make out.

Apparently Bebi couldn't, either. "A shy chap, eh?" He swung back and motioned for us to follow him. "Well, come and visit, and we'll see if we can bring you out of your shell."

"Out of my *shell*?" Khepri squeaked in a tiny, horrified voice that only I could hear.

"Calm down," I said. "He meant he wants you to feel at home."

Bebi had already outpaced us, so I loped ahead to catch up.

CHAPTER 9

The Eye of Horus

Before we entered the next room, Bebi warned me, "We must go quietly through here. The Royal Mother is sleeping."

And so she was. As I slinked across the room, I caught a glimpse of her tiny figure huddled under a fine linen sheet on the low bed. With a sigh, I remembered her glory days, when I was just a young cat and she sat at the side of Pharaoh's father. The flower of Egypt, they called her. Radiant as a goddess, and noble and gracious, just as a Great Wife should be. But when her husband died, all the life went out of her.

An elderly servant, more than half asleep herself, sat on the floor near the bed. Although there were many decorated trunks

piled up against the walls, the room itself was rather plain and small, nowhere near the size of the Great Wife's bedroom, let alone Pharaoh's. Clearly, the Royal Mother had no need of ceremony anymore.

The courtyard where Bebi led us was small as well, and the slight overhang from the roof provided almost no shade. Even the palm trees near the door looked sad, with withered edges on their leaves. There was no pool, either. But right away I spotted what the courtyard *did* have: a large plate of snacks, set beneath one of the palms.

I sniffed at the air. "Bebi, is that roasted duck I smell?"

"Please help yourself," Bebi said. "They brought it to my mistress, and since she wasn't hungry, she offered it to me. But I'm not very hungry, either."

"Well, you know me," I said, sauntering over to the plate. "Always happy to help out."

"Just like your father," Bebi said fondly. "He used to help me that way, too. Those were wonderful days, Ra. When the Royal Mother was the Great Wife, the feasts were never-ending. But all good things must come to an end."

"Er . . . yes." *Including this duck,* I thought. I swallowed a big chunk of it. *Delicious.*

"What about you, Khepri?" Bebi asked. "I expect roasted duck is not to your taste, but over in the far end of the courtyard you might find, er . . . something more to your liking." He pointed discreetly.

Khepri craned over my forehead to see.

"Dung!" he exclaimed in delight. "Why, thank you." To me he whispered, "I guess Bebi really *does* want me to feel at home."

Jumping off my head, Khepri chirped his thanks to Bebi and scampered away.

Bebi smiled at me. "There's no accounting for taste, is there?"

"No," I said. "There certainly isn't." I turned my back so I didn't have to watch Khepri digging in.

Bebi politely averted his gaze, too, and settled himself down beside me. He was careful not to sit too close. He didn't rush me into conversation, either. That's something I like about Bebi—he understands the respect due to Pharaoh's Cat. He's a stickler for the attentions due to rank. Maybe that's because he was pretty high-ranking himself, back in the days when his human was the Great Wife.

After I signaled that I was ready for conversation, however, he was more than happy to start us off. "Tell me, how are things in the palace, Ra? I daresay you know quite a bit more than I do, now that I'm confined to these rooms."

"You're confined?" I hadn't heard this. "On whose orders?"

"Haven't you heard? The Great Wife has a horror of baboons. It seems a brother of hers was attacked by one. The guards are under orders not to let me out unless I'm on a chain and the Royal Mother accompanies me. And since I loathe chains and the Royal Mother rarely leaves these quarters, I spend almost all my time in here."

"Really?" I was shocked. "That's dreadful, Bebi. Something ought to be done—"

"Oh, it's not so bad." Bebi smoothed down a tuft of fur. "Truth be told, I don't know that I'd want to stroll around even if I could. The palace isn't what it used to be, Ra. Besides, my joints can't take the wear and tear. A pity, but there it is. I'm content enough here, believe me. It's a peaceful place, and the Royal Mother is kind. But I do enjoy hearing news from outside when I have visitors."

"Have you heard about the robbery?" I asked, licking my chops. "Someone stole an amulet from the Great Wife this morning."

"The Eye of Horus? Yes, one of the servants came and told us." Bebi shook his silver-maned head. "Shocking, isn't it? The Royal Mother was very upset. That was her favorite amulet."

"If it was her favorite, why did she give it to the Great Wife?"

Bebi looked at me in surprise. "Because she had to, Ra. Pharaoh said it was meant only for a Great Wife to wear—and since his mother was no longer the Great Wife, but a widow, it must be passed on. Just as her great bedroom had to be passed on, and half her possessions." Bebi shrugged in resignation. "It can't be helped. It's how it's always been done. The Royal Mother understood that, but she was worried that the new Great Wife wouldn't treat her things with the care they deserved. And she was right, because now the Eye of Horus is gone. You can imagine how angry the Royal Mother is."

I nosed around for another bit of duck. "Well, you can't really blame the Great Wife if a thief decided to rob her."

"It wouldn't have happened to my mistress," Bebi said stubbornly. "She never let that amulet out of her sight."

"So you remember what this Eye of Horus looks like?" I asked.

"Oh, yes. The Royal Mother used to wear it all the time, even when she was sleeping." Bebi closed his eyes. "It's on a thick gold chain—a gold pendant as big as my hand, with a large eye in the center made of ivory and lapis lazuli."

"Lapis lazuli," I repeated. "The blue stones from the East?"

"Yes, of the very best type. Very valuable," said Bebi. "On one side of the eye stands the vulture goddess Nekhbet, guardian of Upper Egypt. On the other side is the cobra goddess Wadjet, guardian of Lower Egypt. Both of them are studded with turquoise and carnelian stones." He opened his eyes and regarded me sadly. "It is an amulet fit for a queen, Ra, and it protected my mistress from all evils."

Gulping a last scrap of duck, I tried to picture the amulet and memorize the details. "So the gods are turquoise blue and carnelian red?"

"Yes." Bebi scratched his head in puzzlement. "Ra, I don't understand. Why do you care so much about what the amulet looks like?"

"Because I'm going to find it." I cleaned my whiskers with a flourish as Bebi stared at me. "You see before you Ra the Mighty, Pharaoh's Cat and Great Detective."

"And his scarab sidekick," Khepri piped up behind me. He nodded happily at Bebi. "Thank you very much for the dung."

"My pleasure." Bebi looked a little confused as Khepri sat beside me. "Do you mean you two are trying to find the thief?"

"That's right," Khepri and I chorused.

Bebi still looked confused. "But aren't Pharaoh's guards doing that?"

"Yes," I said, "but they're after the wrong person."

Bebi tilted his shaggy head. "And how do you know that?"

Khepri and I looked at each other.

"It's a long story," I said.

We ended up telling Bebi everything.

"What a terrible miscarriage of justice!" he said when we finished. "So that innocent girl is hiding in a storeroom while the real thief gets away with the crime?"

"No need to worry," I assured him. "I'm on the case. And I always get my man."

"How can you always get your man?" Khepri wanted to know. "This is the first time you've ever detected anything, Ra."

"I always *will* get my man," I amended.

Bebi scratched his head. "Ra, my dear fellow, please don't take this the wrong way. But are you sure it's possible for a cat to solve this case?"

CHAPTER 10

The Cause of Ma'at

How could Bebi doubt my abilities? I hopped up from the ground. "Of course it's possible for a cat to solve this case, Bebi. Maybe not *any* cat, but it'll be a breeze for Pharaoh's Cat."

"And for his beetle sidekick," added Khepri quickly.

"Even so—" Bebi began.

"The girl Tedimut appealed to me," I interrupted. "She asked me to save her. It was a direct request, Bebi. To me, Pharaoh's Cat." I thought of the girl's bright eyes and how she'd called me Great One. "It's a *duty*, Bebi. She's depending on me."

"And me," Khepri chirped. "And Miu."

"But mostly me," I said to Bebi.

"Well, it certainly does seem wrong that the girl should be blamed for all this." Bebi squinted down at both of us, his brown eyes almost lost in his fringe of silver fur. "And far be it from me to discourage you, Ra. I admire your desire to serve the cause of justice and truth, the cause of Ma'at."

I held my head up with the kind of pride only cats can muster, my whiskers glinting in the fierce sunlight. The very survival of the universe, and the defeat of chaos, depended on Ma'at—the ideal of harmony and order and balance. Ma'at was what every pharaoh was supposed to strive for. But it wasn't every Pharaoh's Cat who came to his aid.

Pharaoh was trying hard to be a just ruler. Since he came to the throne, he had spent hours every day settling disputes, investigating corruption, and doing whatever the gods required to bring peace and prosperity to the kingdom. But because he was so busy, he sometimes missed important details. He was only human, after all. That's why he needed a cat like me.

"Of course I will do all I can to help you." Bebi nodded at me kindly. "I may not get out much, but I still have some influence, and I hear things now and again that might be useful. Tell me, who are your chief suspects?"

"Er . . . I'm not sure we have any yet," I had to admit.

"Your main lines of inquiry?"

"We don't have any of those, either," I said. "But we know the Great Wife's ladies and servants aren't guilty, because they were all in the Great Wife's rooms when Tedimut was attacked."

"Actually," Khepri said in a small voice, "I was wondering about that."

"You were?" I was surprised.

Khepri raised his bumpy head. "Well, Tedimut said it was Lady Shepenupet's responsibility to make sure the proper jewelry was brought from the treasure room. So what I was wondering is this: Did someone in the treasure room send the wrong amulet by mistake? Or was it Lady Shepenupet who ordered the wrong one—on purpose?"

"Why would she do that?" I couldn't follow Khepri at all. "She'd only have to send it back."

"That's my point," Khepri said. "Lady Shepenupet would have known all along she was going to send the amulet back with Tedimut. That means she could have warned someone else to attack her. I'm not saying it happened that way, but it's a possibility."

Hmmm . . . I hadn't thought of that. Of course, only a truly sneaky person would play such a trick. But after my experience with the tunic and the funny-smelling meat in my bowl, Lady Shepenupet seemed sneaky enough to do just about anything.

Bebi gave Khepri an admiring nod. "Well done, old chap. You really *are* coming out of your shell."

Khepri winced. "I prefer to think of it as coming into my own."

"As you wish, old chap. Either way, it's a pretty piece of reasoning." Bebi turned to me. "You're wise in your choice of partner, Ra."

"Not partner," I reminded Bebi. "Sidekick." But Bebi didn't hear me. He was too busy listening to Khepri.

"So how do we find out if Lady Shepenupet ordered the wrong amulet on purpose?" Khepri was saying. "I don't think Aat knows. But even if she did, she'd never tell us."

"Aat has always been difficult," Bebi agreed. "But what if you tackled the problem from the other end?"

What other end? I was mystified.

Khepri, however, was clicking in an excited way. "You mean we should look for Lady Shepenupet's partner in crime? We could try to find out whether anyone close to her was behaving suspiciously this morning—"

Bebi beamed at him. "My, but you really are a quick-witted chap. Yes, that's exactly what I mean. I can't say I know Lady Shepenupet well, but I did know her father. He was one of the old pharaoh's closest advisers, though I always thought he was a bit slippery. His son—and the brother of Lady Shepenupet—is the Overseer of the Royal Residence. And I believe the Director of the Royal Loincloths is one of their cousins."

The Director of the Royal Loincloths?

Lady Shepenupet couldn't have been plotting anything with him, I thought. He was too nice. But the Overseer—now, that was a definite possibility.

Not only did the Overseer kick me when no one was around, but he also had a liking for fine jewelry. More than once, I'd caught him in the treasure room staring at the royal diadems. It was his job to check on them, I suppose. But he liked to stay there an awfully long time—and he looked at the gold the way I look at a bowl of roasted quail.

"We'll check them both out," Khepri promised. He seemed to have completely forgotten his fear of Bebi. More importantly, he'd forgotten which one of us was the Great Detective.

I rose to my feet. It was time I reminded everyone who was in charge of this investigation. "We need to go, Bebi, but we'll definitely keep your information in mind— along with all our other leads."

Khepri hopped over to me. "We have other leads?"

"Of course we do." Well, maybe not leads, exactly. But *ideas*. I tapped my head with my paw. "It's all up here, Khepri."

"I'd love to hear more," Bebi said.

Khepri waved his forelegs. "So would I."

"Later." I motioned to Khepri to climb aboard. "I appreciate your help, Bebi, but time's moving on, and we need to get back on the trail."

Bebi looked disappointed. He shuffled behind us as we crossed back through his mistress's shabby rooms. "I must say I'm sorry to see you go. I haven't had such an exciting visit in a long time. But good luck to you both. Please do let me know if there's anything else you need." He gestured to the guards by the door, who were moving into place to block his way out. "As you can see, I'm limited in what I can do, but I'll gladly help in whatever way I can."

After we said our good-byes and walked away, Khepri whispered, "He may be a baboon, but he's awfully nice."

"I told you so," I said.

"His dung is nice, too," Khepri added.

I stopped short. "I did *not* need to know that, Khepri."

"And it was warm—"

"Not listening." I picked up my pace. "Not listening. Not listening."

I bounded forward so fast that my hind

legs started to skid. As I careened through the next doorway, my paws went out from under me.

"Watch out!" Khepri cried.

As I rolled to my feet, I heard a snarl behind me.

Babycakes

Yikes! It was Aat. How had she gotten loose?

There was no time to worry about that now. As Khepri scrambled down into my belly fur, I tried to bound away. It was no good. Aat whipped around and blocked the doorway, trapping me between her paws. Her huge amber eyes didn't blink as they held mine.

"What are you doing here, Fluffball?" she growled. "I told you to go back to your pool."

The pool had never sounded better than it did right now. "Er . . . I was just taking a walk."

"Hah!" She bared her teeth. "What do you think I am, Fluffball? Stupid? You peppered me with questions this morning, and now you're nosing around some more. You're up to something. Something to do with the Eye of Horus. What is it?"

Instead of answering, I tilted my head to one side so I could see her collar more clearly.

Whew! Aat wasn't loose after all. Her collar was attached to her chain, and the chain was fastened around a pillar. That meant things weren't quite as bad as I'd thought. Though since we were right between Aat's paws, they were still pretty bad.

How could I get us out of here?

"I asked you a question, Fluffball." This time Aat's growl made my fur ripple. "What are you up to—you and that little decoration of yours? You're not hiding the thief who took the amulet, are you? You'd better tell me now, or I'll slice that nose right off your face."

She was getting too close to the truth, but I tried not to show it. "I told you, Aat. I was just curious."

Her claws shot out. For an instant, I thought my nose was gone. But even as her paw came whistling down, I heard Khepri shout, "I'll save you, Ra!"

He leaped onto Aat's paw and raced up her fur.

"Ewww!" She reared back, dancing around like one of Pharaoh's acrobats. "It's a bug. A bug! Get it off me!" She tried to bat Khepri away. But as I could have told her, he was too clever and quick for that. As I shot out of Aat's reach, he ran straight to the top of her head.

"Get off!" she shrieked. "Go away!" She tried to claw at him, but she only succeeded in nicking her own ear. While she nursed it, Khepri jumped off and scrambled over to me. Once he was on board, I ran into the next room.

Aat howled.

Lady Shepenupet rushed into the room, her peevish face looking alarmed. "Oh, Babycakes," she crooned to Aat. "What's wrong?"

"Babycakes?" I said to Khepri. "Is that what Lady Shepenupet calls her?"

"Looks like it." Khepri giggled.

"Hey, Babycakes," I called back to Aat.

She growled. "Don't you ever, ever call me that."

"Oh, I wouldn't dream of it." To Khepri I whispered, "Babycakes!"

"I heard that!" Aat roared.

"There, there," Lady Shepenupet soothed Aat. "Don't let that nasty cat bother you, Babycakes. You're much, much prettier." Glaring down at me, she fluttered her hands. "Shoo!"

I took my time leaving. "Bye-bye, Baby-cakes."

Khepri and I giggled.

"You'll pay for this," Aat called after me. "The next time I'm off the leash, I'll find out what you're up to. And then you'll be sorry you ever crossed me."

She snarled again to show she meant business, but by then Khepri and I were halfway across the next room. Before long we were completely out of earshot.

Once we were at a safe distance, Khepri and I almost fell over ourselves laughing. "It's serious, though," Khepri said at last. "Maybe we shouldn't have teased her. Next time we see her, she'll be madder than ever."

"Then let's not see her anytime soon," I said. "But don't worry. You're more than a match for her. Thank you for leaping in to save my nose."

Khepri peered down from his perch between my ears. "She didn't hurt you?"

"Not a scratch. She pulled back as soon as you jumped on her." I shook my head, still amazed he had done it. "I never expected you to take her on, Khepri. She's a hundred times your size."

"Wasn't she funny?" Khepri said cheerfully. He hopped down my back, imitating Aat. "'Oooh! Oooh! Get it off me! Get it off me!'"

We both started laughing once more.

"Well, thank you again," I said. "It was a

 102

brave thing to do. Especially when you're just the sidekick."

Khepri didn't look as pleased as I thought he would. "Right." He perched himself on my tail. "I've been thinking about that, Ra. How about we switch? You can be the sidekick for a while, and I'll be the Great Detective."

"Er . . . no," I said. "It's too late, Khepri."

Khepri hopped off my tail. "Too late? Why?"

"Because I've already cracked this case. This is a time for action. Come on, let's go investigate the guilty parties."

"And who would they be?" Khepri asked.

"We already said, didn't we? The Overseer. Lady Shepenupet."

"We said they *might* be guilty," Khepri reminded me. "We don't know for sure. Not yet."

"I have a feeling they're the ones," I said. "And my instincts are always right."

Khepri looked a little cross. "Instincts aren't evidence, Ra. Not even yours. The truth is, it could be just about anybody."

"That's why I'm depending on instinct,"

I said. "If we investigate everyone, this case is going to take forever. And I've missed enough snacks already."

Before Khepri could say anything else, Miu padded out of the shadows, startling both of us.

CHAPTER 12

Bad News

Miu was good at keeping a low profile. I had to give that to her. She'd hidden in the shadows like she was part of them.

"There you are!" She bounded up to us with a little chirrup. "Tedimut's asleep, so I thought I'd see if I could find you. How is the case going?"

"It's going great," I said.

Khepri's click was uncertain. "I don't know about *great*, but we've learned a few things." He told Miu everything we'd discovered so far.

"That's all you know?" Miu said when he'd finished. "I was hoping for more."

"There's nothing to complain about," I protested. "We have our prime suspects—"

"Shhhh!" Khepri warned. "Humans coming."

As we darted into the recess behind a statue of the falcon god Horus, I heard the Overseer coming toward us, speaking in a low voice to his companion, the Director of the Royal Loincloths.

"I don't want any more of your excuses, do you hear?" The Overseer sounded crabbier than ever. "When I give an order, I expect you to carry it out."

"Yes, my lord." The Director of the Royal Loincloths came into view, looking miserable. "It's just that there are complications—"

"Complications?" the Overseer hissed. "What sort? Do you mean blackmail?"

"No, no, my lord." The Director looked more distressed than ever. "I mean that it's difficult for me—"

"And you think it isn't for the rest of us? I've told you what you need to do. *Get it done.*" The Overseer swept away, leaving the Director standing on his own in the middle of the room.

Peeking out from behind the tail feathers of the Horus statue, we all watched him.

"He doesn't look happy," Khepri whispered. "I wonder what the Overseer ordered him to do."

"And why the Overseer mentioned blackmail," I said.

"Maybe it's something to do with the theft," Miu murmured. "Didn't that baboon say the Director was related to Lady Shepenupet?"

"Yes. And to the Overseer," Khepri said.

"Well, maybe all three of them are in it together," Miu suggested.

Now, that was a ridiculous idea. "The Director wouldn't steal anything," I told her. "He's not the type."

"Look at him," Miu urged. "That's a guilty face if I ever saw one."

The Director certainly did look troubled. Instead of running off to follow the Overseer's orders, he was sighing heavily and shaking his head.

"I think it's time for some purring," Miu told me. "Why don't you give it a try?"

She wanted me to fawn over the Director and make a fool of myself? No, thank you. "He's innocent, Miu. And anyway, he's not part of my family."

"But you know him. He's your friend. Isn't it worth a try, for Tedimut's sake?"

I sat back on my haunches. Tedimut could count on me for everything else, but not that. I was giving all I had to this case— even missing my snacks!—but Pharaoh's Cat had to uphold his royal dignity.

Miu sighed in exasperation. "All right, then. I'll do it myself." She darted out of our hiding place, twined around the Director's legs, and started to purr.

The Director brightened. "Oho! It's the Beloved One, yes? You're still here?" He reached down and stroked the back of her head.

Miu's purr grew louder.

"It's not a good day for me, cat," the Director told her. "Not a good day at all. Everywhere I see trouble." He looked as if he were about to cry.

Miu stretched out under his hand, purring and twisting and generally acting like a half-grown kitten. Honestly, I was embarrassed for her.

"I'm not supposed to go around talking about it," the Director whispered, "but I guess you won't say anything, will you, cat?

The Overseer says I have to act quickly, but he doesn't understand what's involved. I feel so guilty—" He pulled back his hand. "Uh-oh, you'd better disappear, cat. I think someone else is coming after me."

After Miu raced back to us, Lady Nefrubity came in to talk to the Director. As usual, her eyes were so deeply rimmed in kohl that she looked half raven. She whispered in the Director's ear. I couldn't make out a single word, but he looked more troubled than ever as they passed out of the room.

"That looks suspicious to me," Miu said. "Let's follow them!"

I skulked behind the statue. "Wait a minute, Miu. I hear marching. And clanking. Something's going on."

"He's right," Khepri agreed. "It sounds like Pharaoh's guards. And they're coming our way."

Echoing against the brick walls of the palace, the clanking grew louder. Moments later, the guards jogged past us, spears in hand, their sandaled feet dark with dust. In their wake several scribes followed, talking excitedly.

"Is it true the guards have found the thief?" one asked.

"That's what I heard," another scribe replied.

"May it be so," a third added.

Miu gasped.

Khepri heaved a tiny sigh of distress.

I stopped in my tracks. Were they talking about Tedimut?

Uh-oh.

"We must go quickly," the first scribe said, clutching his writing tablet. "They're

going to report to Pharaoh in the audience hall, and he may want us there to take
notes."

They hurried down the hall. As soon as
the coast was clear, we raced after them,
moving so fast that our paws hardly
touched the ground.

CHAPTER 13

Pharaoh

When I attend one of Pharaoh's audiences, I usually go in style. Once the lamps are lit and the horns are sounded, I mount the dais with Pharaoh and pose on the top stair. That way the crowd gets a chance to admire me before I take my place under the throne. It's just how we do things around here.

But not today.

By the time we got to the audience hall, it was already full of people, and none of them noticed me. To be honest, I was a bit disappointed. But a Great Detective is great whether people notice him or not—and I suppose sometimes it's best if they don't.

My main worry at that moment was Tedimut, and I was relieved not to see her as

Miu and I pushed our way to the front of the crowd. A few people shuffled back when we skirted past their ankles, but no one looked down. They were too busy listening to Pharaoh.

Not that you have to listen too carefully. Pharaoh has a voice as deep and loud as a lion's. "Where is the amulet?" he demanded of the guards. "Where is the thief?"

The chief of the guards flinched and dropped to his knees. "O Ruler of Rulers, Keeper of Harmony and Balance, Lord of the Two Crowns, we have searched half the town, but we have not found them—yet."

High on his throne, glittering in his golden collar and double crown, Pharaoh frowned.

I've had the chance to observe many of Pharaoh's frowns up close. The ones I know best are of the "Ra-you've-been-a-naughty-cat" variety—where you meow once or twice, and everything's fine. This one went well beyond that. This one meant business.

"You have failed me," Pharaoh said, grim as the Nile before it floods.

The officer turned a shade of gray. "O

Ruler of Rulers, we live only to serve you. We will find the amulet, I promise—and the thief. We have guards stationed at every door and wall of the palace, and all around the town. We will search every hiding place. She cannot escape us."

"See that she does not," Pharaoh said, still grim. "That jewel is a treasure of our royal house, and we are pained by its loss. Its theft is not only a betrayal. It is treason. The thief shall be punished accordingly."

With his powerful arms, he lifted the crook and flail of royal office—a signal that the audience was over. To show their respect, the crowd prostrated themselves on the floor. It felt strange not to mount the dais and enjoy their admiration as I usually did. But I was a Great Detective now, and I had a job to do. When Miu shot out of the hall, I followed her.

"Did you hear that?" she said to me as soon as we reached an empty room. "Pharaoh said the theft is treason. And the punishment for treason is death." Her eyes were wide with panic. "It was just a piece of jewelry, Ra."

PHARAoh

"Not to him," I said, but I shuffled my paws uncomfortably. Truth be told, I agreed with her. A piece of jewelry wasn't worth someone's life.

The trouble was, when Pharaoh first came to the throne, he'd been determined to be merciful. (This was a change from his father, who'd been about as merciful as a pillar of granite.) Unfortunately, some noblemen had taken Pharaoh's mercy for weakness, and they plotted to overthrow him. Since then, Pharaoh had taken a harder line, starting with the noblemen themselves. He was determined to keep order, whatever the cost. Quite right, too: a Pharaoh who can't keep order can't serve Ma'at.

But I wasn't too happy with him right now, even if I didn't want to say so to Miu. Tedimut wasn't a powerful nobleman or a fearsome enemy. She was just a child. Even if she was guilty, she didn't deserve to die— and I was ready to stake my royal honor that she was innocent.

"Don't worry," I said, as much to myself as to Miu. "It won't come to that. We all know Tedimut didn't steal anything."

"But Pharaoh thinks she did." Miu glanced at Khepri and me with imploring eyes. "You two have to solve this crime. Do you hear me? You have to keep Tedimut safe."

Who was Miu to command me to do anything? I scratched my right flank. "Well, we'll do what we can—"

"You *have* to," Miu repeated. "Start by investigating the Director of the Royal Loincloths. He's up to something. I know he is."

I didn't move so much as a whisker. Pharaoh's Cat doesn't take orders from anyone.

"And what about you?" Khepri asked her.

"I need to get back to Tedimut," Miu said. "If she wakes and I'm not there, she might be afraid. And with all those guards looking for her, I have to make sure she stays quiet. But if you ask me, the key to this mystery is that Director. He even said he was guilty, remember?"

"He said he *felt* guilty," I corrected. "There's a difference." At least, I hoped there was.

"You're splitting cat hairs." Already Miu was pulling away from us. "Don't let him go!"

I didn't like the idea of taking orders from Miu, and I really didn't think the Director of the Royal Loincloths had stolen the amulet. Yet I was uneasy with what we'd seen and heard earlier. What exactly did the Director feel guilty about? After a little persuasion from Khepri, I agreed to investigate further.

When we found the Director, he was by himself in Pharaoh's robing room, kneeling by an open chest.

"Oh, dear." He rubbed his shaven cheeks. "Oh, dear."

"What's he so upset about?" Khepri whispered.

"Let's find out," I said, and bounded over to him.

At the sound of my paws, the Director slammed the chest closed and turned. He relaxed when he saw it was just me. "What are you doing in here, Ra? Looking for your

Beloved One?" He rose to his feet. "I saw her a little while ago, back near the feasting room."

I rolled my eyes and padded over to the chest. Why had he slammed the lid down? Was there something inside it?

"You should go out to the pool," the Director said, straightening his sash. "Maybe that's where your Beloved One has gone."

Hmmm. . . . Was he trying to get rid of me?

Before I could figure out the answer, several young servants walked in, and the Director went off with them. I decided to stay with the chest.

"We're not going to be able to open it, Ra," Khepri said.

"You just watch," I told him.

I pushed at the chest. I clawed at the lid. When that didn't work, I started to yowl.

Two servants came running.

"It's Pharaoh's Cat," the taller one said as I stood on the chest. "He sounds upset."

"Maybe there's something wrong with that chest," the smaller one said. "A mouse inside it, perhaps? We'd better take a look."

While Khepri and I watched, they opened the lid. When I walked toward them, they backed away, bowing. With Khepri holding on tight, I jumped into the chest.

It held half a dozen of Pharaoh's second-best loincloths. And absolutely nothing else.

After that, Khepri and I found a quiet corner. I stretched out on the tiles, and Khepri jumped down, looking discouraged.

I was feeling a little discouraged myself. I'd spent hours running around the palace, missing a whole afternoon by the pool, and for what? I needed a break. "Hey, Khepri, what do you say we go get some snacks?"

"Snacks?" Khepri looked at me in disbelief. "Ra, we just ate. Over at Bebi's, remember?"

I did, but remembering only made me hungrier. "That feels like a long time ago."

"Well, it's not. And anyway, we can't afford to take a break," Khepri said. "There must be about a thousand people in this palace, and I don't see how we're going to investigate them all. It's hard enough checking up on our chief suspects."

The way Khepri was talking, our investigations were going to last for *days*. But I wanted this case solved fast. Preferably before suppertime. And judging from the angle of the light coming through the windows above us, suppertime was almost here.

Suddenly an idea came to me—a truly great one, if I do say so myself.

"I know just what to do," I told Khepri.

He looked surprised. "You do?"

"Yes. Climb aboard."

With a small sigh, Khepri sidled onto my back. "Can you at least tell me where we're going?"

"Hold on tight," I said. "We're going to visit the biggest gossips in Egypt."

CHAPTER 14

Gossip Central

It was a good thing Khepri did hang on tight, because I was moving fast. We needed to get this case solved quickly, so I took every shortcut.

As I pulled through a gap that wasn't much bigger than I was, Khepri shouted, "Hey! You nearly knocked my head off."

"Sorry," I said, but I didn't slow down. My gossips kept early hours. If I didn't hurry, they'd be bedded down for the evening, and we wouldn't get a word of sense out of them.

When I came to a halt outside a half-open door, Khepri moaned and dropped down dizzily onto the floor. "Next time remind me to skip the ride," he said. "I'll use my own six legs."

"Don't be silly," I said. "It would've taken you till tomorrow to get here."

"Maybe that wouldn't have been so bad." Khepri gazed at the door in front of us. "Where are we, anyway? Have we been here before?"

"We're just outside the schoolroom," I said. "The place where they tutor the royal sons and their companions. Well, the older sons, anyway. The youngest is only a baby."

Khepri looked confused. "Is that who your gossips are? The children?"

"Oh, no." I marched through the open door and past a row of benches. "The children are done with their lessons by now."

Khepri scuttled behind me. "Then why are we here?"

Instead of answering, I sat myself down next to a stack of stone tablets and gazed up at a wall decorated with paintings of baboon-headed Thoth, the god of writing and knowledge. "Yoo-hoo! Ini, Ibi, are you here?"

My caterwaul echoed in the quiet room, but everything remained still.

"Looks like they're not at home," Khepri said.

"Wait!" I pointed with my paw. "Look up there."

Two heads peered down from an opening halfway up the wall, right above Thoth's head.

"Who-oo is it?" Ini called back, and then she saw me. Her beak flashed as she turned to her brother. "Ibi, it's Ra the Mighty." She sang down to me, "We'll be right with you-oo."

"Yikes!" Quick as a whistle, Khepri dashed under my belly. "They're birds! Why didn't you tell me, Ra?"

"Does it matter?" I said.

"Yes," he hissed. "Birds eat beetles."

"Not these birds," I assured him. "They're the Prince's pet turtledoves, and they get all their meals on a tray. They'd never go after a live beetle—especially not my friend." I thought this over. "Well, Ini wouldn't, anyway. She has very nice manners."

Khepri didn't move away from my belly. "What about the other one?"

"Ibi?" I said. "I wouldn't worry about

him, either. After all, you're a bit too big for a turtledove beak."

"Good to know," Khepri said, but he stayed where he was.

"Really, Khepri, you're fine. I'm a cat, remember? Ini and Ibi are friends of mine, but they tend to keep their distance all the same. You're perfectly safe."

"I hope you're right about that." Cautiously, Khepri emerged into the open, just in time to see Ini spread her tan-and-black wings and flutter down to the bench above us. Ibi was right behind her.

"Greetings, Ra the Mighty!" Ini bobbed her gray head at me, motioning to her brother to pay his respects, too. "What brings you-oo here? We usually only see you-oo at the pool."

I was about to answer when I noticed that Ibi's amber eye was fixed on Khepri.

Khepri noticed, too. He drew back with a nervous click.

Ibi's beak opened wide. "Who-oo's that?" he asked me.

"This is Khepri." I put one paw on either side of him, just so Ibi knew where we stood. "He's a friend."

Ibi snapped his beak shut. "Too-oo bad," he sighed.

"He's helping me out," I went on.

"Helping with what?" Ini ruffled her feathers in curiosity. "What's going on, Ra?"

"It's about the amulet that was stolen from the Great Wife," I said.

"Oo-oo," cooed Ini excitedly. "We've been talking about that all day. The humans say the girl Tedimut took it, but Ibi and I don't think so."

"You don't?" I said. "Why not?"

"She's a good girl," Ini said.

"We used to watch her when she worked in the kitchens," Ibi added, finally taking his eye off Khepri. "She always gave us crumbs."

"We never once saw her take something that wasn't hers," Ini said. "And we see a *lot*." She fluttered her tail feathers proudly. "Please, tell us everything you-oo know."

I didn't want to tell the biggest gossips in the palace that we knew where Tedimut was. One word to them, and before long everyone from the Princesses' caged canaries to Pharaoh's hunting dogs would know Tedimut's hiding place.

"Well, actually," I said, "I was wondering what *you* know. You hear everything, don't you? And you're always up early. Maybe you even saw the whole thing happen?"

"No," Ibi said regretfully. "We missed it."

"But only just," Ini said. "We were out and about then. In fact, I was perched right by the treasure room when the Eye of Horus went out to the Great Wife."

Khepri jumped up with excitement, though he was careful to stay close to my paws. "An eyewitness at the treasure room! That's just what we need."

Both birds stared at him.

"You-oo do-oo?" Ini said in surprise.

"Yes," I said. "Do you happen to know if the treasure room guards sent the Eye of Horus by mistake? Or did Lady Shepenupet ask for it specifically?"

"Oh, it wasn't Lady Shepenupet who-oo went to the treasure room," Ini told me. "She made Lady Nefrubity do her fetching and carrying this morning. But I did hear Lady Nefrubity say that Lady Shepenupet wanted the Eye of Horus."

Hmmmm, I thought. Were we after the wrong person? Was it Lady Nefrubity who had hatched a plan to steal the amulet?

That would be an unexpected development. After all, except for her kohl-laden eyes, you wouldn't look twice at Lady Nefrubity. Not only did she have no real power, but she also never called attention to herself, and nobody had much to say about her. But then, wasn't that the hallmark of the greatest master criminals—their ability to look perfectly harmless?

"I was so surprised to hear Lady Nefrubity ask for the Eye," Ini went on. "It belonged to the Royal Mother, and she and the Great Wife don't get along."

"You-oo can understand it on the Royal Mother's side," Ibi put in. "Think of all she had to give up—those beautiful rooms and some of her servants and so much of her jewelry. But I don't understand why the Great Wife couldn't be more gracious. She never says anything nice about the Royal Mother. She even makes jokes about her."

It was true. I'd heard those jokes myself. But the Great Wife joked about everybody—except Pharaoh, of course.

"And I saw with my own eyes how the Great Wife wrinkled her nose the last time her ladies dressed her in that amulet," Ibi went on.

Ini nodded. "She made such a fuss about it. Between you-oo and me, I thought her ladies would never bring it out again."

"Maybe Lady Nefrubity forgot what she was supposed to ask for," Ibi suggested. "She has a terrible memory, you-oo know."

Khepri and I looked at each other. Maybe it had been an innocent mistake, then. Or maybe not.

"Did you notice anything else unusual before dawn this morning?" Khepri called up to the doves. "Was there anyone who wasn't where they should be? Or anyone behaving strangely?"

The two turtledoves conferred, wings rustling.

"Not just one person," Ini said at last. "There were several. After I left the treasure room, I saw the Overseer running across the audience chamber. He's usually at the temple at that hour."

The Overseer! I could well believe he'd been up to no good. "When was that, exactly?"

"Right before the hunt for the girl started," Ini said. "I remember all the shouting."

"And just before then, I saw the Director of the Royal Loincloths skulking near the Great Wife's rooms," Ibi added eagerly. "He should have been in Pharaoh's robing room."

I didn't like the sound of that, so I did my best to ignore it. I heard a little whirr from Khepri, though, which meant he was thinking hard.

"And then there's Yuya, the children's tutor," Ini said. "He was late getting to the schoolroom, and he's been jumpy as a gazelle all day."

"It could be that he's short of money again," Ibi put in. "I heard him asking Lady Nefrubity for help yesterday. She's his aunt. She told him she would help pay off his debts, but only if he stopped gambling."

Khepri had stopped whirring. "Did she say anything else to him?" he wanted to know.

"Not that I heard," Ibi said. "That's when the servants brought in our food, so I missed the rest."

I could sympathize with that. In my experience, it's hard to pay attention to anything else when there are snacks in front of you. In fact, just hearing Ibi mention food was enough to make me start wondering what would be on my dinner plate tonight.

Khepri, however, was still full of questions. "What kind of man is this Yuya? Is he bold or timid? Weak or strong? Honest or shifty?"

"You-oo can see for yourself." Ini cocked her head toward the doorway. "He's coming now. I can tell by the footsteps."

Khepri raced up to my head to get a better view. I stretched out my neck, because I was curious, too. Yuya had been appointed royal tutor a few months ago, but I'd not yet had any dealings with him.

A young man stepped through the doorway. Ibi was right: he really was jumpy. He was biting his lips and breathing fast, and his gaze darted all around the schoolroom before landing on me.

"Scat! Get out of here, cat!" He drew his foot back to kick me.

CHAPTER 15

Yuya

Yuya's heavy foot almost struck me, but I was too fast for him. I sailed through the doorway, Khepri clinging to my fur.

"See you later," I called out to Ini and Ibi. "Come find me if you see anything else suspicious!"

Yuya appeared in the doorway. "Get out of here, you nuisance."

Nuisance? Didn't he know who I was?

Apparently not, because he picked up a sharp stylus and raised it like a dart.

"Hey, those are for writing, not throwing!" I shouted, but he hurled it at me anyway.

Luckily it struck the tile floor, but I saw

he had another one in his hand. I stuck out my tongue and raced away.

"Well, that was very interesting," Khepri said once we were out of danger.

I stopped in midstride. "Interesting? Is that what you call it? Khepri, the man almost broke my ribs."

"He never had a chance," Khepri said. "You were too quick."

That was true. I felt a glow of pride. I was more than a match for that mummy-brain.

"But he certainly did want you out of there," Khepri said thoughtfully. "The question is why?"

"Because he's a lousy excuse for a tutor," I said. "People like that shouldn't be allowed to teach children. They set a bad example."

Come to think of it, maybe that was why the royal sons had been a bit rough with me of late. Frankly, I preferred the way Tedimut treated me. Now, there was someone who set a *good* example.

"Maybe Yuya thought you were trying to attack the Prince's doves," Khepri said.

"I wasn't anywhere near them!" Well, no closer than a foot or two.

"Or maybe he has something to hide," Khepri said. "Something he doesn't want anyone to know about, even Pharaoh's Cat."

"*Especially* Pharaoh's Cat." Aha! All the pieces were falling into place. "But it didn't work, Khepri. Because I see now that he's guilty. He's the one who took the amulet—"

"I didn't say that," Khepri interrupted.

"I know you didn't. I did. I'm the Great Detective, remember? Yuya's obviously the kind of lowlife who would steal anything. And think of what Ini said about his aunt, Lady Nefrubity. She must be the person who helped him."

"Not so fast, Ra." Khepri slid down to the floor. "The way I see it, we have at least three suspects. Well, three teams of suspects, anyway. I think we should go over the case against each of them before we come to any hasty decisions about who's guilty."

"It's not a hasty decision," I grumbled, "not when the answer is staring us in the face."

"Humor me," said Khepri. "There's Yuya and Lady Nefrubity, yes? Lady Nefrubity was the one who asked the treasure room for the Eye of Horus. So she could have warned Yuya that it would be sent back there, and he could have ambushed Tedimut in the hallway."

"And that's exactly what he did," I said. "The brute."

"Maybe," Khepri said. "But why?"

"For the gold and the jewels," I said. "He needs to settle his debts. That's what he said to Lady Nefrubity yesterday. Ibi heard him."

"But Ibi says Lady Nefrubity told Yuya to stop gambling. That doesn't sound like someone who was about to help him commit a crime."

"It was a cover-up," I suggested. "She offered to pay Yuya's debts, remember? And

I don't think she has much money. Maybe she has some savings I don't know about, but probably she was going to get what she needed by stealing the amulet."

Khepri looked doubtful. "You think she would stoop to robbery to help her nephew?"

"If anyone would, it's Lady Nefrubity. Aat said she never stops talking about her nieces and nephews. She's obsessed with her family."

"But Lady Nefrubity wouldn't have known it was Tedimut who would be sent back with the amulet. So she couldn't have told Yuya who to attack," Khepri objected. "It was Lady Shepenupet who decided that. So maybe it's Lady Shepenupet who's at the bottom of the plot. She couldn't have stolen the jewel herself—she was in the Great Wife's bedroom when it happened—but maybe she was working with the Overseer or the Director. Or both."

"It wasn't the Director," I said, but I was a little uneasy. I'd forgotten how good the case against Lady Shepenupet was. And it was true that the Director had said he felt guilty.

"Presumably they would have stolen it for the money, too," Khepri said. "Lady Shepenupet and the Director are connected to all sorts of wealthy people, and some of them might pay well for something as precious as the Eye of Horus. It could only be worn in secret, of course. Unless they broke it apart for the gold and jewels."

I wasn't used to having to think so hard. My head was spinning. "Are those all our suspects, then?"

"No, there's one more." Khepri hesitated.

"Who's that?" I asked.

Khepri quickly glanced around the dark hall we were in, as if he were afraid someone might be listening. Coming close to my paw, he lowered his voice and told me a name I hadn't expected to hear.

CHAPTER 16

The Last Suspect

"The last suspect is the Great Wife herself," Khepri said softly. "We know she hated the amulet. Plus, she's in need of money."

"The Great Wife needs money?" I was startled. "Says who?"

"I've heard them talking about it in the stables," Khepri said. "My very favorite spot, the stables." He gave a happy little sigh. "So much dung."

"Enough about the dung," I said. "What did you hear about the Great Wife?"

"That she spends more than she should. She showers her favorites with gifts—"

"And who could blame her for that?" I said. "Personally, I find it delightful." *Especially when that favorite is me.*

"—and she likes her luxuries," Khepri went on. "I mean, just look at that bedroom of hers. Gold everywhere! No wonder she has trouble keeping to her allowance. They say she used to be able to talk Pharaoh into giving her more, but Pharaoh is growing stricter about money. One of the grooms overheard the Great Wife complaining about it to one of her ladies."

Hmmm . . . I'd certainly heard that Pharaoh was trying to keep a closer eye on expenses. His father and the Royal Mother had spent lavishly, but Pharaoh kept saying that times were different now. Thankfully, he wasn't cutting back on my snacks, so I'd thought no more of it. But maybe the Great Wife had more reason to be concerned.

"What if the Great Wife was upset that she wasn't getting the riches that the Royal Mother had enjoyed?" Khepri speculated. "And what if she saw the amulet as a solution to her problems? Maybe she persuaded the Director or the Overseer or Yuya—or someone we don't know—to stage a theft. Once the fuss dies down, she could sell the amulet, or even melt it down. It's a crime to do that behind Pharaoh's back, of course. Only Pharaoh can dispose of the royal jewelry. But he would never know."

I twitched my tail. I didn't like this line of talk. After all, the Great Wife had been known to feed me from her own plate—a sign of good character if there ever was one. And she was *Pharaoh's* Great Wife, so she was part of my family. I needed to defend her.

"Aat told us that the Great Wife likes Tedimut," I pointed out to Khepri. "So why would she let Tedimut get blamed—and have guards hunting her down?"

"From all I hear, the royal family isn't as concerned about their servants as you seem to think," Khepri said.

My fur rose. "What are you talking about?"

"I'm saying the family takes their servants for granted," Khepri said calmly. "They don't spend much time thinking about the people who make their lives so easy. If they lose a cook or a gardener or a sandal-bearer, they just get a new one."

There was an uncomfortable pause. Uncomfortable for me, anyway. I didn't like admitting it, but Khepri had a point. I'd seen plenty of servants come and go in my time, and no one in the royal family ever cried about it.

"It's better than it used to be," was all I could say. "The old pharaoh and the Royal Mother were much harder on the servants. People say Pharaoh is a kinder master. And of course the Great Wife is more generous—"

"Maybe to her favorites," Khepri cut in. "Like Aat."

I winced at the mention of Aat. "Okay, okay. So the Great Wife's judgment isn't always perfect, I'll grant you that. But she's not cruel, Khepri. And she'd have to be vicious to pin the crime on Tedimut and let her suffer the consequences."

"Maybe she meant for Tedimut to be found knocked out on the floor," Khepri suggested. "That way it would be clear that the girl was the thief's victim, and she wouldn't be punished. The Great Wife probably didn't plan for Tedimut to run away."

"You're trying too hard." Talking about all these motives was making my head hurt.

"Why do we need to consider so many suspects, anyway? I'll bet you anything Yuya's hiding that amulet in the schoolroom right now. That's why he chased me away."

"I'm not sure about that," Khepri said. "We don't know if he's guilty. But I agree: we probably should check on him." He clambered onto me. "Turn around, Ra."

"Now?" I shook my head. "Khepri, he'll only chase me out again. We'll go back later tonight, when the coast is clear." *And after I've had some snacks.*

"And what if Yuya takes the amulet out of the schoolroom before then?" Khepri asked.

"Then Ini and Ibi will follow him," I said. "I told them to tell me if anything suspicious happened."

"And what if they fall asleep?"

He had a point. Ini and Ibi weren't at their best at night.

"Oh, fine," I grumbled. "We'll go now."

As we retraced our route, all I could think about at first was my tail, and how I didn't want it broken. But then my hunting instincts kicked in, and I started to get excited. If we were lucky, we'd catch the thief right in the act. Tedimut's name would be cleared, and I'd be a hero!

When we reached the schoolroom, the doors were bolted shut.

Khepri tried to crawl through the gap underneath them, but it was too narrow. "I think Yuya might be in there, though," he reported. "I heard something rustling."

"That could be Ini and Ibi." I bent down to the crack and called out to them. No one replied, but I did hear rustling.

"He's in there, and he's locked us out." I paced beside the doors. "So what do we do now?"

"Is there any other way in?" Khepri asked.

"Only a tiny opening up high for the doves," I said. "I couldn't get through even if I somehow got up there. And a human certainly couldn't."

"Then we wait here," Khepri said, "until Yuya comes out."

Waiting turned out to be harder than I thought. The longer we stood in front of those doors, the worse I felt. My whiskers drooped. My paws ached. My stomach rumbled.

"I'm hungry," I told Khepri.

"We'll eat as soon as this is over," Khepri promised.

That didn't sound soon enough to me. "Maybe I'll just dash back to the pool and see what's for dinner."

"Okay," Khepri said. "Go ahead. I don't mind being the Great Detective for a while."

"Oh, no," I said. "Wherever I am, I'm still the Great Detective."

"Not if I'm the one who finds the amulet, solves the crime, and saves Tedimut," said Khepri.

That was hard to argue with, even for me. I sat myself down. "I guess I'm not so hungry after all."

But of course I *was* hungry—and tired. Khepri seemed tired, too. When I curled up by the wall, he settled down in the crook of my tail with a sigh.

He nodded at the door. "Let's hope Yuya comes out soon."

We waited some more, but nothing happened, and I started to think about food again. I imagined myself stretched out by the pool, the sun warm on my fur, a plate of yummy roasted quail in front of me. With maybe a few morsels of stewed antelope on the side . . .

I closed my eyes for a moment to picture the plate more clearly. Before I knew it, I'd fallen asleep.

An outraged whisper jerked me out of my dreams. "Ra! Khepri!"

I opened my eyes. Khepri scrambled to his feet.

Miu stood before us, eyes blazing. "I don't believe this. I was hoping you'd solved the crime. And here you are, fast asleep!"

"No, no, no." I stifled a yawn. "We're not sleeping. We're watching. We're guarding the schoolroom doors." I pointed at them.

I blinked. The doors were now slightly ajar.

"Uh-oh!" Khepri and I exclaimed.

We ran to the doors.

The schoolroom was empty.

CHAPTER 17

Searching for Answers

"He got away!" I shouted.

"It sure looks like it," Khepri said.

Miu came up behind us. "Who got away? What are you talking about?"

"Yuya," I said. "The royal tutor. He's the one who stole the amulet, and now he's taken it somewhere."

"We don't know that for sure," Khepri said. "Maybe he didn't steal it in the first place. Or if he did, maybe he left it here."

I ignored the first part of what he said. But the second part made sense. "You're right, maybe it's still here. Let's search for it—and let's track Yuya down."

"We can't do both at once," Khepri said.

"Sure we can. We just need reinforcements." I leaped onto a bench. "Ini! Ibi! Wake up! Come help us!"

Ini poked her head out. "What is it?" she asked sleepily. "What are you-oo doing back here, Ra? It's the middle of the night."

I had no real idea what time it was, but it was true that everything was very dark and quiet. Khepri and I must have slept for hours.

Ibi appeared beside his sister. "Ra, who-oo's that strange cat with you-oo?"

I made quick introductions. (Pharaoh's Cat knows how to handle all social situations, no matter how complicated. I'm just like Pharaoh himself in that way. It's part of our mystique.) After a bit of chittering between themselves and a few wary looks at Miu, Ini and Ibi came down.

As they settled on a bench that was a fair distance from us, I briefly explained the situation, and Khepri began to fire off questions. The birds couldn't hear him very well, so I repeated them. "How long did Yuya stay, and what did he do while he was here? And where did he go afterward?"

"I wish we knew-oo," Ini said. "But we were both asleep."

"You, too?" Miu could barely contain her frustration. "What's wrong with you all? Am I the only one awake on the job?"

Khepri gave her a warning click. "Please don't be so critical, Miu. We need their help."

"Just like you need ours," I pointed out.

Miu sighed. "All right. But please, can you stop talking and *do* something?"

"We were getting to that before you interrupted us," I said. "Ini, Ibi, can you check the palace for Yuya? We need to know where he is. If you find him, one of you should stay with him, and the other should come back here and get us."

Ini and Ibi complained a bit because they didn't like flying around the palace at night. But I'm very persuasive, if I do say so myself, and finally they flew off.

"Now for the treasure hunt!" I said. "Let's see if the amulet is still here."

"If it was ever here at all," Khepri said cautiously.

As I've mentioned before, Khepri has

trouble looking at things optimistically But I didn't let that bother me. It was only after we searched every square cubit of the classroom—every tablet, every stylus, every scroll—that I grew discouraged. There was no sign of the amulet anywhere.

"He must have taken it with him," I said.

"If it was ever here at all," Khepri said again.

Just then, Ini and Ibi flew back into the schoolroom.

"Yuya's in his bed," Ini reported.

"Fast asleep," Ibi added.

"And now we're going to bed, too-oo," they chorused.

As they retreated to their nest, Khepri sighed. "So we haven't seen any sign of the amulet, and Yuya's in his bed, just where he should be. I think we're on the wrong track."

I wasn't giving up. "I still think Yuya's up to something. Let's see what he does. I'll get Ini and Ibi to keep an eye on him all week—"

"All week!" Miu's eyes blazed again. "Is that your plan? What about Tedimut? She can't stay put for a week. I managed to fetch her some grapes today, but they won't last long. I can't believe I trusted you to solve this crime. I need to find a way to get her out of here."

"I can solve it," I said. "Just give me a little more time."

"I don't *have* time," Miu said. "Tedimut is thirsty *now*. She's hungry *now*. And it's only going to get worse." She turned to go. "If I'm going to get her out of here, I'd better do it tonight, while she has the strength to climb and run."

It hurt to think of Tedimut going hungry and thirsty. It wasn't right that the child should suffer so. But it wouldn't help her if we behaved rashly. "You can't do that, Miu. You'll never get her past the guards."

"I'll tell you what I can't do." Miu drew herself up, and for just a moment she looked like the goddess Bastet, not just an ordinary kitchen cat. "I can't let Tedimut waste away in that storage room while you two doze off and pretend to solve the crime."

"We're not pretending!" I said indignantly.

"Wait!" Khepri cried.

But Miu vanished through the doorway, running as fast as she could back to Tedimut.

CHAPTER 18

Going Somewhere?

"Does she mean it?" I said to Khepri. "Is she really going try to get Tedimut out of here all by herself?"

"I think that's exactly what she's going to do," said Khepri. "She's a very determined cat."

I shook my head. "I don't care how determined she is. She'll never get past Pharaoh's guards."

"That's why we need to stop her." Khepri clambered up my back. "Come on, Ra."

I didn't budge. "Stop her? How are we going to do that? She won't listen to us."

"Maybe she won't, but if you bar the way, Tedimut will stay put." Khepri settled himself between my ears. "She won't go against

Pharaoh's Cat. Of all the creatures in the palace, she'll pay heed to you. It's almost as good as having Pharaoh himself. Maybe even better."

"You're right," I said, brightening.

"But we have to find her more to eat and drink." Khepri sounded worried. "Miu's right. She won't last long in that storeroom without help. What if I brought her some dung? There's some really tasty stuff over by the stables—"

I could just imagine Tedimut's face. "Not a good idea, Khepri."

"No, I suppose not. People don't appreciate good dung the way they should." Khepri tapped the ground in thought. "I know. We could bring her some of your snacks."

"My *snacks*?" Did I hear that right? I'd been on the case for hours, and now Khepri was seriously suggesting I give away my food?

On the other hand, Miu had said the child was hungry. All day in that storeroom, with only a few grapes to eat . . .

"It would be a very noble thing to do," Khepri said. "Almost godlike. Like Bastet herself."

I had to admit I liked the sound of that. And I wouldn't mind hearing the child call me Great One again.

Besides, if I said yes, I could go get my snacks *right now*. Saving some for Tedimut, of course—but who could blame me if I ate plenty myself? A Great Detective has to keep his strength up somehow.

"Okay," I said. "We can bring Tedimut a little snack. Let's go back and see what they've left out for me."

We set off through the dim, quiet palace. The closer we got to Pharaoh's quarters, the faster I ran. What would the snacks be? Licking my lips, I imagined them. Quail. Spiced antelope. And if I was lucky, maybe some broiled goose on the side.

I was so busy thinking about food that I forgot to check the shadows and didn't listen for the sound of someone creeping up behind me. I wasn't even paying much attention to the route we were taking.

Khepri piped up, "Hey, isn't this the room where Lady Shepenupet left Aat?"

I laughed. "You mean Babycakes?"

"I told you never to call me that!" Out of

the shadows, Aat sprang at us, teeth bared.

With a yowl, I bolted, dodging her claws by a whisker. She chased me into the audience hall, and I dashed for the canopy above Pharaoh's throne. Aat was too heavy to follow me there, but she waited for me down on the floor.

Tail bristling, I peered over the edge at her.

Now, you may think that, sitting on top of a flimsy canopy, in the dark, with an angry leopard threatening to kill me, I might be scared. But I am Ra the Mighty, Pharaoh's Cat, as brave as a lion and twice as fierce. Still, I must admit it was a challenge to be fearless with Aat's sharp teeth gleaming brighter than her golden collar.

"I'm going to deal with you once and for all," she snarled, her eyes glowing. "And that disgusting little bug of yours, too."

"Disgusting?" Khepri whispered indignantly in my ear. "Let me at her, Ra! I'll show her what's what."

I shook my head. Khepri had managed to fend off Aat before, but he'd been lucky in his timing, and now he wouldn't have surprise on his side. What if he slipped and Aat crushed him? I didn't want him to risk it.

"No need," I whispered back. "I've got this."

What we needed was a distraction. The only way I could create one was by talking, but maybe that would be enough.

"Hey, Aat," I called out. "You're looking a little underdressed."

Her tail twitched suspiciously. "What do you mean?"

"Your chain," I said. "I miss it."

"I don't."

"What happened?" I persisted. "Did it break?"

"You have your secrets, Fluffball. I have mine."

I blinked. "You mean it *didn't* break?"

"I'm not saying anything," Aat growled. "But maybe I'm not the only one around here who wants that thief dealt with. And maybe I'm not the only one who's tired of you poking your nose where it doesn't belong. You ask too many questions, Fluffball."

With that, Aat sprang up at me. I leaped back, but not fast enough. She pinned me by my tail and pulled me down off the canopy.

"Got you, Fluffball!" Her breath was hot on my fur. "Now I get even."

Khepri launched himself at Aat. "Take that, you big bully!"

With her free paw, Aat knocked him out of the air. He landed wrong side up.

As he wriggled his legs in the air, she laughed. "I'll deal with you later, bug."

I looked at Khepri, horrified. What had Aat done to my friend? Cracked his shell? Knocked off his pincers?

Fury gave me a strength I didn't know I had. I ripped away from Aat, leaving shreds of fur in her claws. In one swift move, I scooped up Khepri with my mouth and dashed out the nearest doorway.

"Not disaaaay!" Khepri called from my open mouth.

He can speak! I thought. But I couldn't make sense of what he'd said. And Aat was hot on my trail.

I was moving like lightning, but in the

end a leopard can always outrun even the speediest of palace cats. I needed a place to hide—and when I saw a familiar-looking statue with a frieze above it, I knew I'd found it. Aat would have trouble following me up there; she was too big to use the paw-holds on the statue.

I reached the top of the frieze just before Aat came into the room. Lowering my head so she couldn't see me, I let Khepri out of my mouth.

In case you ever are tempted to put a dung beetle in your mouth, let me give you a piece of advice: don't. It's not just that they taste rather, well . . . dunglike. They also tickle.

At any rate, Khepri's legs tickled me—and when he wriggled his way out, the tickle got unbearable. I sneezed.

Below us, Aat growled. She knew where we were.

And then it hit me what Khepri had actually said: *Not this way.*

I'd brought Aat straight to the place where Miu had picked up Tedimut's scent.

Uh-oh.

As Khepri scrambled onto my back, I watched Aat size up the distance between us. I'd been right that she couldn't get up here using the statue. But it turned out she didn't need to. In a single great bound, she leaped up to the frieze, landing right in front of me.

"Going somewhere?" she snarled.

"Yes!" I flung myself down to the floor, twisting through the air and landing upright. For once, I was hoping Aat would follow me. Anything to keep her from hunting down Tedimut.

Aat sniffed at the frieze.

"Hey, Babycakes!" I yelled. "I'm down here!"

Aat put her head out the window. "The thief!" she roared, and she jumped out onto the roof.

CHAPTER 19

Just a Cat

Khepri and I stared up at the window. Even during the worst moments of the day, I'd been sure that I would crack this case. But not now. Not when it looked like Aat would polish off the case in her own way—putting an end to Tedimut.

"We've got to stop her!" I cried.

"But how?" Khepri clutched at the fur on my head, as frantic as I was. "Aat will get to the storeroom before we will."

"She'll never get through that tiny vent," I said, remembering the horrible splinters the grate had given me. "She'll have to find another way through, and that will take a while."

"To the storerooms, Ra!" Khepri said. "If

we're quick, we can get to Tedimut and Miu first and warn them."

I'd already started running. "What if they've already left?"

"They won't have gotten far," Khepri said. "There hasn't been enough time."

He was wrong about that. We came across Tedimut and Miu much sooner than we expected, crouched in a passageway on the far side of the audience hall. Tedimut looked exhausted, and her shoulders were hunched with fear.

As I brushed against her legs, she let out a startled gasp. I moved to a moonlit patch of floor, and she recognized me. "Pharaoh's Cat!" she whispered, bowing her head. "O Great One, please help us!"

"That's what I'm trying to do," I said to Miu. "But you're making it difficult. I thought you were trying to get Tedimut out of the palace, not deeper into it."

"I am." Miu sounded frazzled. "I've been trying to lead her to the break in the wall by your pool. That's how I came in, and I believe Tedimut is small enough to get out that way, too. But I don't know the

165

palace very well, and Tedimut can't see in the dark, and we got lost and almost ran into a guard. Now she's so tired I don't think she can go a step farther."

She nudged her head against Tedimut's back, urging her onward. Tedimut stayed put, her head still bent. She seemed to be shaking with cold, even though the night was hot.

"Uh-oh," said Khepri.

Tedimut was at breaking point.

I wished I had the kind of magic she needed, the kind of magic she expected Pharaoh's Cat to have. I wanted to be like my ancestor Ra, defending the righteous and smiting the powers of chaos and evil. But there in the dark, I had to face the hard truth: even if people treat you like a god, that doesn't make you one. I hated to admit it, but Khepri was right. In the end, I was just a cat.

Yet maybe being a cat was enough. Or could be, if I set aside my dignity and did whatever was needed to get Tedimut moving again.

I stepped forward and brushed against

Tedimut's side. When she didn't respond, I rolled over onto my back, squirming with my paws in the air. I knew I looked absolutely ridiculous—and in front of Miu, too—but I didn't care. Thinking only of Tedimut, I let out the loudest purr I dared.

"Great One?" Tedimut whispered.

I flipped over again, planted my front paws on her knee, and licked her face.

"Come along, child," I breathed. "You can do this."

She couldn't understand my words, but she must have felt their strength. She raised her head and met my eyes. Her face brightened. And when I pulled away, she rose and followed me.

"Oh, thank the gods!" cried Miu, catching up to us. I waited for her to make a crack about my lack of dignity, but she added quietly, "And thank you, Ra."

I was so surprised I didn't know what to say.

"Where are we going?" Miu asked.

"To the pool. Your plan was a good one." If she could bring herself to thank me, then I guessed I could be polite, too. And it was true: the wall by the pool probably *was* the best way out. "Come on, we need to pick up speed. And keep the sound down. Aat's on our trail."

"The Great Wife's leopard?" Miu whispered, appalled. "Don't they keep her chained?"

"Someone let her loose," Khepri said in his tiny voice.

"Well, that's what she wanted us to think, anyway." I steered us down a passageway that led away from the sleeping quarters. With two cats to guide her, Tedimut could move faster now. For a human, she was quite fleet of foot. "Maybe it was just talk."

"I don't think so," Khepri said. "Didn't you see her collar? There weren't any bits of chain attached to it. And if she'd broken away, the collar would've been scratched and bent. Gold that pure dents easily—"

"I'm not sure," Miu interrupted, "but I think I just heard a roar in the distance."

I heard it, too, and I think Tedimut did as well, because her body tensed. Now she knew just what we were up against. But she didn't cry out, and she didn't crumple into a ball. She kept following me, as brave as a cat.

"It's Aat, but it sounds like she's still on the roof," I said to Miu. "She's probably trying to get into the storerooms." I quickened my pace, and so did the others.

"So who do you think released her?" I said softly to Khepri as we turned down the passageway that led to the pool. "Lady Nefrubity? Lady Shepenupet? Yuya?"

"Probably not Yuya, since the doves saw him asleep," Khepri said. "Besides, it would be hard for a tutor to sneak into the Great Wife's quarters to do it. Lady Nefrubity and Lady Shepenupet seem a lot more likely."

"I bet it's Lady Shepenupet," I said. "She's never liked me."

"That doesn't have anything to do with it, Ra," Khepri argued. "Everything isn't always about you, you know. Even if you are Pharaoh's Cat."

"But Aat said it *was* about me, didn't she?" We reached the doorway that opened onto the pool. "She said she wasn't the only one tired of me snooping around and asking—"

"That's it!" Khepri shrieked in my ear as we passed through the doorway and entered the courtyard. "Ra, that's the solution!"

So it *was* Lady Shepenupet?

"*Yeeeooooooooowwwwwwllllllll!*"

With a cry like a demon, Aat sprang down from the roof and attacked us.

Last Chance

Spitting and snarling, Aat dropped down, trapping us at one end of the pool. Tedimut screamed, but she didn't run.

"Good girl," I said. Running wasn't a wise idea with a leopard.

The trouble was, staying still wasn't a wise idea, either.

Baring her dagger-sharp teeth, Aat swung her head toward Tedimut.

I hadn't gotten the girl this far to lose her now. Springing between them, I screeched at Aat, "Don't touch the girl!"

Miu jumped in front of me. "That's right! Don't touch her!"

"Don't tell me what I can and can't do," Aat roared. "We play this game by *my* rules.

This time none of you are getting away. Now who shall I take first? You, Fluffball? Or this lying, thieving girl?" Tail lashing, she fixed her eyes on each one of us in turn.

A light flared in a palace window.

"Jump into the pool!" Khepri whispered into my ear. "Leopards can't swim."

"Yes, they can," I whispered back. Khepri clearly didn't know leopards at all. "It's cats like me who can't."

"Well, then you stay out. But get Tedimut in." Khepri shifted back from my ear. "I have a plan."

He sounded very sure of himself. And it was true that the pool was our only possible path to the gap in the wall, now that Aat was blocking the other way. Besides, I knew that the pool wasn't very deep, not by human standards. It probably wasn't over Tedimut's head, even if it was over mine.

"Here we go!" I cried. Twisting myself against Tedimut's legs, I tipped her into the pool. A neat job, if I do say so myself—except that I tipped myself into the water, too.

Khepri leaped off me just in time. The next thing I knew, Aat was dancing madly round and round, screaming, "Get that horrible bug off me!"

"Escape while you . . . *burble* . . . can!" I gasped at Tedimut, trying to claw my way back to land.

She didn't understand me, of course. But she was already sloshing her way to freedom.

While Aat was distracted by Khepri, the way to the wall was clear. Miu had dashed past the shrieking leopard and was standing there on the other side of the pool, waiting to guide Tedimut to the exit.

"*Aaaaaarrrrrrrgh!*" I flailed at the water as it closed over my head.

Tedimut was already moving toward Miu, but when she heard me, she turned back. The next thing I knew, she was plucking me out of the water.

But her kindness cost her dearly.

Behind us, Aat growled. She was at the edge of the pool. Had she thrown off Khepri? Had she killed him?

Dripping wet in Tedimut's arms, I yowled in alarm. Licking her lips, Aat crouched, ready to spring on us.

"*Stop.*"

It was the voice of Pharaoh. And in Egypt, everyone listens to Pharaoh. We all froze, even Aat.

Magnificent in his embroidered night robes, Pharaoh appeared in the doorway.

An instant later, his guards raced forward.

Sssssssssssssswish! A net went down over Aat.

I started to cheer, but then two of the guards leaped into the pool to seize Tedimut.

"It's the girl!" the first guard called back to the others. "The thief who stole the Great Wife's amulet."

"Looks like she was trying to steal Pharaoh's Cat, too," the second guard said, prying me from Tedimut's arms. He set me gently on the side of the pool. "Or drown him."

"I would never do that!" Tedimut cried, turning to Pharaoh. "O Ruler of Rulers, I would never do any of it!"

"Of course she wouldn't," I spluttered. As always, however, none of the humans understood me. Not even Pharaoh.

"Tie her up, and set a watch over her," Pharaoh ordered. "We will deal with her in the morning."

I could guess where that would lead. At best, Tedimut would find her nose cut off. At worst—if the charge of treason held— she would be sentenced to death.

"You've got the wrong thief!" I mewed.

"He certainly does," someone whispered from under my belly.

"Khepri!" I'd never been happier to hear his voice. "Are you all right?"

"I'm fine," Khepri said, climbing aboard. "Aat did her best, but she can't stop me. We've got to save Tedimut."

"I'm trying," I said. "But they just won't listen." Pharaoh was talking to his guards about Aat, held captive in the net. No one seemed to notice I was there, except Aat herself, who snarled at me.

"Never mind," Khepri said. "I've got a plan."

I was a little wary, given that Khepri's last plan had nearly drowned me. "What is it?"

"Steal something from Pharaoh. His beads, his sash, his slipper—I don't care what."

"Me? Steal from Pharaoh?" I balked. "Khepri, really. We royals don't do that kind of thing to one another."

"It's not impossible," Khepri said grimly. "Just make sure he notices."

"Khepri!"

"Trust me," Khepri said. *"Now."*

I only had to think about it for a moment. The truth was, I did trust Khepri. Maybe I hadn't when we started this detective job, before we'd had to work together as a team. But I did now.

Brushing up against Pharaoh's knees, I clamped my teeth on the end of his gold-embroidered sash. Jerking it free, I started running, the sash spooling out behind me.

"Ra!" Pharaoh called out. "Bring that back! This is no time for games."

"To the audience hall!" Khepri shouted in my ear, and I raced ahead.

Behind us, I heard Pharaoh shouting, and the heavy footsteps of guards chasing after us.

"Slow down just a little," Khepri said. "We need to make sure the guards follow us. There, that's it. Go!"

I was too winded to ask where we were going, but I wouldn't have anyway. I didn't want to admit to Khepri that I still didn't know for certain who the thief was. But I was pretty sure that it was Lady Shepenupet.

When we reached the audience hall, Khepri told me where we were really going.

I couldn't say anything because my mouth was full of sash. (And an awful mouthful it was, too. Gold threads are so prickly.) But I could hardly believe what he said.

And yet, as I thought it over, it made a funny sort of sense.

"Run!" Khepri said. "They're catching up to us!"

With the guards right on my heels, I raced through the palace, trailing drops of water from my soaked fur as I ran. Leaping over several servant women and waking them from sleep, I arrived at the final door. It was closed, but not latched, and when I pushed against it, it opened onto a shabby room lit by a single candle.

As the guards tumbled in behind me, the Royal Mother put up a startled hand. Even in the faint light, the Eye of Horus glittered brightly over her heart.

CHAPTER 21

A Higher Justice

I stared at the Eye of Horus. The amulet matched Bebi's description perfectly—an enormous eye made of gold and ivory and lapis lazuli, with gods in turquoise and carnelian on each side. And here was Pharaoh's mother wearing it.

"Ra, what possessed you?" Pharaoh came through the door. He stopped dead when he saw the amulet. "Mother? Where did you get that?"

"Maybe the girl gave it to the Honored Royal Mother, O Ruler of Rulers," a guard suggested.

Pharaoh's mother gave the guard a withering glance. "A girl? What are you talking about? It was my precious baboon who brought this back to me. My sweet Bebi, who serves me always."

The guards looked staggered, but not as staggered as Pharaoh.

"*Bebi* did this?" Eyebrows sky-high, Pharaoh looked from the baboon to his mother. "I don't believe it."

"He's a very clever creature, my Bebi," the Royal Mother said calmly. "All I had to do was let him out into the courtyard and he went up the palm tree onto the roof. From there, he crept into the Great Wife's rooms—the rooms that used to be ours—and he took back what was mine." She motioned to the darkest corner of the room. "Come here, Bebi darling."

Shuffling out of the shadows, the old baboon joined her, candlelight shining on his silver hair.

As Pharaoh and his mother began to argue, I stalked up to Bebi.

"Bebi, how could you?" I said, shocked. "I thought you cared about justice. About Ma'at."

"I do," Bebi said, with angry dignity. "I serve Ma'at—and the Royal Mother. Pharaoh has treated her shamefully. His own mother! He made her give up everything to the new Great Wife, and the new Great Wife never showed her a single kindness. It wasn't fair, Ra. It wasn't just."

"It's the way things have always been done," I said.

"It wasn't fair," Bebi repeated. "So when I found a way into the Great Wife's quarters, I knew it was meant to be. I started retrieving the Royal Mother's favorite treasures—first, her beads and her comb. And then, when I saw it, the Eye of Horus. It wasn't stealing. It was taking back what was ours."

"But you knocked Tedimut on the head to get the amulet," Khepri pointed out.

"It was merely a small stone," Bebi muttered, avoiding our eyes. "I was serving a higher justice."

"And you set Aat on us," I said.

"I only told her to scare you off. And I didn't set her after the girl."

"But you must have known Aat would get carried away," I said. "You know what she's like—"

"I was serving Ma'at," Bebi said stubbornly. He wouldn't look at us. "I was doing what was right, and you were getting in the way. I had to do something."

Khepri clicked disapprovingly. I shook my head. Alongside us, Pharaoh was scolding his mother, who was nursing the amulet against her heart. When Bebi leaned against her, she stroked his silver hair. "Bebi knows what is owed to me," she crooned. "Bebi is always loyal and true. Unlike certain others." She glared at her son.

Pharaoh looked pained. "Mother, that's not fair."

"You neglect me. You do. You don't care about me!" She clutched the Eye of Horus. "Your father had this made for me—for *me*! And you took it away." She bent her head and started to cry.

Pharaoh touched a hand to her shoulder, then turned to his guards. "You will go now. You will not speak of this matter to others, but you will release the girl. Make sure everyone knows she is innocent and under my protection."

My tail soared. Never let it be said that Pharaoh can't learn from his mistakes. His father could never admit to being wrong, but Pharaoh's different. He always wants to set things right. Unlike Bebi, he's a true servant of Ma'at—even if he does need a little help sometimes.

After the guards left, Pharaoh picked up the sash I'd taken from him, and bent down to stroke my damp head. "You may go, too, Ra. I don't know how you knew. But thank you."

I leaned into his hand, rubbing my cheek against his palm. *You're welcome.*

When Pharaoh finally stood up and turned away, Khepri jumped onto my back. Bebi still wouldn't look at us. There was no point in saying good-bye.

As the door closed behind us, I heard Pharaoh say, "Now, Mother . . ."

Pharaoh's Cat is as fast as they come, but that night's adventures had exhausted me. With Khepri riding on my head, I padded very slowly back through the palace, stopping now and again to snaffle up various crumbs lying around. Normally, I'd be more particular, but after so much exertion I needed all the nourishment I could get.

At the entrance to the Great Wife's rooms, I paused. For once, it wasn't for treats. I stopped because I'd heard a young girl's excited voice.

"Tedimut!" Khepri cried.

Wanting to see for myself that she was safe, I marched—well, waddled—through the doorway.

When Tedimut saw me, she beamed. "There he is, O Gracious Great Wife," she said to the radiant queen stretched out on the gilded divan. "Ra the Mighty, Pharaoh's Cat, Protector of the Small, and Defender of Justice. He solved the crime, and he saved my life."

"Ra solved a crime?" The Great Wife tilted her elegant head and half-smiled, as if she thought Tedimut was joking.

"I don't see how that can possibly be true," Lady Shepenupet sniffed.

Lady Nefrubity blinked her kohl-rimmed eyes at me. "I thought all he did was eat."

Honestly. I'd missed a day's worth of

snacks in the pursuit of justice, and this was the thanks I got?

"I don't know how he did it," Tedimut admitted. "But the guards say he did, and I believe them." She looked at me, eyes shining. "Pharaoh's Cat can do anything."

I was touched, I have to admit it. What a discerning child.

Behind me, a guard spoke up. "The girl speaks the truth, O Gracious Great Wife. Ra the Mighty did solve the crime. I saw it. I was there."

"And I, too," another guard added.

"And I," a third chimed in. "He led us straight to the culprit."

"How extraordinary!" exclaimed the Great Wife. Lady Shepenupet looked unnerved, and so did Lady Nefrubity. As I swished my way past them, they regarded me with new respect.

About time, I thought.

When I took a spot near Tedimut, the Great Wife smiled at me, and then at the guards. "Tell me, can you confirm the rumor I heard? That the Royal Mother is the guilty one?"

"We cannot speak to that, O Gracious Great Wife," the first guard said with a stolid expression. "As I said, we were sent here only to return the girl Tedimut to your most gracious charge. The Ruler of Rulers says she is innocent and under his protection."

"I see." The Great Wife gave a knowing look to her ladies, then turned back to the guards. "And is it true, what Tedimut told me about the leopard Aat?" she asked anxiously. "That Aat attacked her?"

"Yes, O Gracious Great Wife," the guard said. "It is true."

"I saw it," said the next.

"I was there as well," the third added, holding up his bandaged hand. "And I have the scratches to prove it."

The Great Wife looked more anxious than ever. "So Aat will not be coming back?"

Tedimut stiffened. So did I. Was the Great Wife going to beg Pharaoh for Aat's freedom?

CHAPTER 22

O Great One

"The Ruler of Rulers says that the leopard cannot return to the palace," the guard said. "She attacked the girl, and she attacked the guards who tried to subdue her. She is a danger to all who live here."

"That's ridiculous," Lady Shepenupet said to the Great Wife. "Tedimut probably teased the poor thing."

The Great Wife froze her with a look. "That leopard attacked a child, Lady Shepenupet. How can you defend that? Do you wish my own children to be eaten by Aat?"

Lady Shepenupet turned red and bowed her head. "Of course not, O Gracious Great Wife."

"Come here, dear girl." The Great Wife

beckoned to Tedimut. "I am so very sorry for all you have suffered. We must make it up to you."

She and her ladies began cooing over Tedimut and plying her with delicacies. For a few moments, I lost sight of the girl, but then Tedimut darted through the crowd and ran over to me, carrying a plate of roast duck.

"For you, O Great One," she whispered. She bowed her head as she offered the plate to me.

O Great One. Such wonderful words! And the crispy duck smelled delicious. But even as my mouth watered, something struck me as wrong.

It was the way Tedimut was bowing her head. True, I was Pharaoh's Cat, and I'd rescued her. No wonder she was grateful. But hadn't she rescued me, too, in the pool?

I poked my head forward and nuzzled her fingers.

Tedimut smiled in delight. Her bright eyes met mine, and she reached out and stroked my fur.

I meowed in approval.

Khepri and I were leaving the Great Wife's rooms when we overheard Lady Nefrubity talking to some of the younger servants.

"Terrible, isn't it, that Aat turned on that dear child?" she said. "But I'm not surprised. Felines are untrustworthy, and not just the big ones. Why, a cat once shredded my darling nephew Yuya's entire collection of papyrus rolls. He can't abide the sight of the creatures now."

"So that's why he chased you out," Khepri murmured sleepily in my ear.

Maybe I should stop by the schoolroom more often, I thought.

By the time Khepri and I reached the pool, the moon was rising, but Miu was there waiting for us. I found her beside my sleeping mat. The servants always set it by the pool on hot nights.

"Have you been here this whole time?" I asked her.

"No," Miu said. "First I made sure that the guards released Tedimut and brought her to the Great Wife."

"We went to see Tedimut, too," I said. "We must have just missed you."

"That's because I went to check on Aat. Some of the guards were told to put her in a cage by the stables, and I wanted to see for myself that she couldn't get out."

"And can she?" I asked.

"No," Miu said. "She's locked up tight. They took her jeweled collar away, too. Aat's furious."

"Good." I yawned.

"So tell me what happened," Miu said. "Who was guilty? The guards wouldn't say, and Aat didn't seem to know."

"Pharaoh's mother had the amulet," I told her. "It was Bebi, her baboon, who stole it." I shook my head, still stunned that the thief was Bebi. Bebi, who was my father's old friend. Bebi, who cared so much about justice.

Miu looked surprised and impressed. "And that's why you grabbed the sash? To lead Pharaoh to the true culprits?"

I nodded. Sleepy though I was, I liked

 190

the admiring way she was looking at me.

"But how did you know?" she asked. "How did you solve the crime?"

"Er . . ." The truth was, I was hazy on the details. I waited, hoping Khepri would chime in. After a moment or two, I realized he was asleep.

Miu looked at me expectantly.

"I'll tell you everything in the morning," I said to her. "Right now, I need to rest." Careful not to disturb Khepri, I lowered myself to the sleeping mat and settled my head on my paws.

Miu frowned. "But—"

"In the morning," I said firmly, closing my eyes.

I expected her to go back to the kitchens. To my surprise, however, she lay down beside me. Not right next to me, exactly, but close enough.

I wasn't used to having anyone share my sleeping mat. After a moment or two, however, I decided I rather liked it.

Soon we were all fast asleep.

All too soon, Miu was nudging me with her paws. "Are you going to sleep all morning, Ra?"

"Go away," I moaned, eyes tight shut. "It's the crack of dawn."

"Dawn? The sun's been up for hours," Miu said.

"It's true," chirped Khepri. "And it's a beautiful day, Ra."

I opened my eyes a chink. The sun was high in the sky, and the air was already heavy with heat.

"A beautiful day," I agreed. "Just right for sleeping." I buried my head between my paws.

"Oh, he's hopeless," I heard Miu say. "You can ride on me instead, Khepri."

"Let me try one more time." Khepri tugged at my right paw. "Wake up, Ra! You don't want to miss this."

CHAPTER 23

The Great Detective

"What am I missing?" I said groggily, opening my eyes again.

"Your chance to say good-bye to Bebi," Khepri said.

"Bebi?" That woke me up. "He's going? Where?"

Miu was already running toward an entrance to the palace. "Come on," she called back. "If we don't go now, they'll be gone."

"Hurry, Ra!" Khepri climbed onto my back. "We'll explain as we go."

When we caught up with Miu, they told me everything they'd learned that morning.

"We stopped by the Great Wife's rooms to see Tedimut," Miu said. "They're being kind to her, and she's happy. She had a chance to visit with her uncle Sebni in the kitchens this morning, and they were so glad to see each other. Oh, and Aat is still furious. I heard Pharaoh might send her to his enemies as a gift."

"Some gift!" I said.

"We also found out why the Director of the Royal Loincloths was so worried," Khepri told me. "The Overseer was insisting that he dismiss some of his underservants to save money. The Director hates having to fire anyone, so he kept putting it off. Two of them are cousins to Lady Nefrubity, who kept asking him to promote them, and that made him feel even worse. He couldn't stand their suffering."

"So what will happen?" I asked. "Who will be dismissed?"

"No one," Khepri said. "It turned out Pharaoh didn't know about the Overseer's plans. When Pharaoh heard about them this morning, he said he sees no reason to dismiss loyal servants. He's going to move two of the underservants to his mother's household, and he'll make the rest of the savings elsewhere."

"And that's not all Pharaoh had to say," Miu added. "He ruled that his mother may keep the Eye of Horus. She's also to be given a much better set of rooms."

"But the new rooms will be in a different palace, farther down the Nile," Khepri said. "That should help keep the peace between the Great Wife and the Royal Mother."

"And what about Bebi?" I asked.

"Bebi is going with her, but Pharaoh said he had to be put on a chain," Khepri said. "It's not just because of the stealing. Pharaoh questioned Tedimut and examined her injuries, and he ruled that Bebi can't be trusted around children."

A chain was a terrible thing, but I understood Pharaoh's decision. I was still angry that Bebi had thrown a stone at Tedimut and that he'd used Aat to hunt us down. What made it worse was that Bebi wasn't sorry. He would do anything to help the Royal Mother. I was relieved he was powerless to harm anyone now.

We came out onto the broad steps that led down to the palace's river landing.

"Look." Miu pointed with her paw as

Khepri hopped off my head. "They're leaving."

A boat was leaving the landing, its white sail blinding-bright in the morning sunshine. Under a canopy, in the position of honor, sat Pharaoh's mother. Next to her was Bebi. I could just make out the thick golden chain that now twined through his fur.

I saluted him with my tail, for old friendship's sake. He looked up, and I'm sure he saw me, but he turned his face away.

Being a Great Detective isn't easy. It's hard on the paws and the stomach. It can even cost you a friendship or two. But luckily, it can also teach you who your real friends are. I moved closer to Miu and Khepri, and together we watched the boat sail down the Nile.

When it vanished from sight, Miu turned to me. "Ra, you still haven't told me how you solved the crime."

"Oh, it was easy," I said. "You tell her, Khepri."

"Well, it was Ra who really cracked it," Khepri said.

I had? How? I kept quiet, while trying to look wise.

"Ra was paying attention to exactly what Aat said," Khepri went on. "Someone had freed Aat—that much was clear from her collar. But she gave the game away when she said it was someone who wanted Tedimut caught, who was tired of Ra nosing around and asking questions. That suggested someone was upset about our investigations—upset enough to unleash Aat on Ra. But who knew what we were up to? That's what I asked myself."

Oh! I started to see his point. "Our human suspects didn't know we were doing detective work."

"Right," Khepri agreed. "They have no idea that we can talk to one another, and they didn't suspect that we were trying to solve the crime. But Aat and Bebi and the doves knew we were on the case. So it had to be one of them, or some other animal they'd talked to."

"How did you narrow it down to Bebi?" Miu asked.

"He was the only one with a motive,"

Khepri said. "None of the other animals had any connection with the Eye of Horus, but it used to belong to Bebi's mistress. And I remembered what Aat had said—that the other missing objects were old and not particularly valued by the Great Wife. It occurred to me that maybe they had belonged to Pharaoh's mother, too—and that she and Bebi had wanted them back."

Ah, I thought, *so that's how Khepri knew.*

"I wondered how he got past the guards," Khepri said, "but then I thought about how Aat had attacked us from the roof. Then I remembered the palm trees by the door in Pharaoh's mother's courtyard, and I realized Bebi probably could have used them to reach the roof.

"And there was an even stronger reason why it had to be Bebi," Khepri went on. "Tedimut was attacked by someone who threw a rock at her head. To throw, you have to have hands. And to take Aat off her chain, you needed hands, too. Bebi is the only animal here who has them."

"You see?" I said to Miu, satisfied. "It was obvious."

"Well, I can't say I saw it myself," Miu said, "but then my mind was on Tedimut. I'm so relieved you managed to clear her name." She looked happier than I'd ever seen her. "Hooray for the Great Detective and his sidekick!"

I looked down at Khepri. He didn't seem as pleased with Miu's cheer as you might expect. And I thought I knew why.

"Make that the *two* Great Detectives," I said.

Khepri gave a delighted click. "Yes!"

And what about Miu? After all, she was the one who'd found Tedimut's hiding place. "The *three* Great Detectives," I amended.

Khepri fluttered his wings. "And the three great friends!"

"Hear, hear," Miu meowed.

We all cheered.

Khepri hopped back up to my head. "So what's our next case, Ra?"

"Next case?" I squinted. "You mean you want to do this *again*?"

"Of course!" Khepri said with a bounce. "I've never had so much fun in my life."

Fun? Was he serious? I rolled my eyes.

Miu gave me a cat smile.

Hmmm . . . On the whole, I suppose it *had* been fun.

"Well, maybe we could do it again sometime," I said as we turned to go. "But first—"

I stopped to yawn.

"First what?" Khepri asked.

"Yes, what?" Miu wanted to know.

"First, we have some snacks." With Miu beside me and Khepri on my head, I padded back toward the pool. "And then a nice, long nap."

Ra's Glossary
of Names

Aat (*aht*): A spotted beauty (at least in her own eyes). Watch out for the claws!

Bebi (*beb*-ee): Wise companion of the Royal Mother. My father's old friend (and mine).

Bastet (*bas*-tet): My favorite goddess, paws down. Not to brag, but I'm a direct descendant.

Horus (*hor*-us): Falcon god. Protector of Pharaoh. Owner of a famous eye.

Ibi (*ib*-ee): Frequent flier. Top gossip. Willing to eat almost anything.

Ini (*in*-ee): Also a frequent flier and top gossip, but more picky about food.

Khepri (*kep*-ree): My scarab beetle buddy. As he likes to remind me, it's also the name of a god of creation and renewal.

Ma'at (*mah*-aht): The goddess of balance and justice and truth. All Great Detectives serve Ma'at.

Miu (*mew*): A humble name for a determined cat.

Nefrubity (*nef*-roo-bit-ee): One of the Great Wife's ladies. Look for the one with the most kohl around her eyes.

Nekhbet (*neck*-bet): Vulture goddess and protector of the Pharaoh.

Sebni (*seb*-nee): A cook in Pharaoh's superb kitchens. We've never met, but Miu is fond of him.

Shepenupet (*shep*-eh-noo-pet): Head of the Great Wife's ladies. Fond of Babycakes.

Tawerettenru (*tah*-wah-ret-ten-roo): Another one of the Great Wife's ladies. A real talker.

Tedimut (*ted*-i-mut): Lowly assistant to the Great Wife's ladies. A girl who treats cats with the respect they deserve.

Thebes (*theebs*): Famous for the Temple of Amun, with its hall of enormous columns. Site of the best snacks in the kingdom.

Thoth (*thawth*): God of learning and writing and scribes. In the schoolroom he's shown with the head of a baboon, but sometimes he has the head of an ibis instead.

Wadjet (*wahd*-jet): Snake goddess, usually shown as a cobra. She and Nekhbet often appear together, sometimes next to an Eye of Horus.

Wedjebten (*wed*-jeb-ten): Yet another one of the Great Wife's ladies. (Really, how many people does it take to get dressed in the morning?)

Yuya (*yoo*-yah): Tutor to the royal sons and their companions. Nephew of Lady Nefrubity. No respecter of cats.

Note: No one knows for certain how ancient Egyptian hieroglyphics were pronounced. Even Egyptologists don't know! For example, some pronounce the name Thoth as "*thawth*," while others say "*tawt*"—and there are other possibilities, too.

Author's Note

Stories can start in the strangest places. This one started in the Egyptian Sculpture Gallery of the British Museum, where you can find a statue of Ra and Khepri. If you ever go there, walk toward the back and gaze to your right, and you'll see it in a case all by itself. Just look for the cat wearing an Eye of Horus amulet. The museum calls the statue the Gayer-Anderson Cat, but if you look closely, you'll notice a scarab beetle riding on top of the cat's head. Who else could it be but Ra and Khepri?

Although this story comes from my imagination, it has roots in real history. Wherever possible, I've used actual facts about ancient Egypt to create Ra's world.

Ra is right, for example, in thinking that cats had a special place in ancient Egyptian life. Most Egyptian gods had animal features or an animal form, and the goddess Bastet was almost always shown as a cat or a cat-headed woman. She was a protector of children, the family, and the home, and she could be both gentle and fierce, just like a real cat. A temple in the Egyptian city of Bubastis was devoted to her worship, and priests and pharaohs performed ceremonies to honor her.

The great sun god Ra was sometimes shown as a cat as well, although there was nothing gentle about him. Wielding a ferocious knife, he battled with a serpent that represented the forces of darkness and chaos.

Egyptians also loved ordinary cats. This was partly because cats kept rats from eating their food, but Egyptians seem to have liked cats for their own sake. Tomb builders sketched funny drawings of them on shards of pottery. Painters showed them hunting or curling up under chairs. Sometimes people were even named after cats—

including the pharaoh Pa-miu, whose name meant "tomcat."

As far as I can tell, there was no official position of "Pharaoh's Cat" in ancient Egypt, but cats were certainly kept as pets by Pharaoh and his family. So were leopards, baboons, and turtledoves. Lions, monkeys, falcons, greyhounds, and horses were also popular royal pets. Pharaohs may sometimes have kept antelope, gazelles, ibexes, giraffes, and elephants as well.

No doubt there were scarab beetles at the palace, too. Ancient Egyptians were impressed by the way these beetles rolled dung into huge balls, and by the way the tiny beetle babies emerged from those balls. To Egyptians, scarabs propelling dung balls were like gods helping the sun cross the sky, giving life to all creation. This is why the Egyptian creator god Khepri was almost always depicted as a scarab beetle. Many Egyptians wore scarab-shaped amulets for luck and protection, and a scarab-shaped stone was often placed over a mummy's heart.

What about Ra's snacks? Do those have any basis in fact? Well, yes. Although Egyptians loved animals, they also liked to eat meat. From tomb paintings, grave goods, and written records, we know that pharaohs, their families, and other wealthy Egyptians ate beef, pork, venison, duck, goose, ibex, gazelle, and antelope. They liked their meat boiled, stewed, or roasted with butter and oil (and probably their cats liked it that way, too). They wouldn't touch fish, however, which they considered unclean. Indeed, if you ate fish, you weren't welcome in the palace.

Ordinary Egyptians rarely, if ever, ate meat. Most were poor farmers, and it was often hard for them to make a living, especially in times of drought and famine. They would have considered a girl like Tedimut very lucky. Because she had a job in one of

Pharaoh's palaces, she would always have a place to sleep and food to eat.

By modern standards, Tedimut's life was hard, but most children in ancient Egypt were expected to work, either beside their parents or for others. Only the sons of noblemen and scribes were educated by tutors like Yuya. Children were much loved by their families, but most never learned to read or write, and instead learned skills from their parents or relatives. Farmers' sons learned to farm, fishermen's sons learned to fish, and potters' sons learned to make pots. Daughters were usually taught how to run a household, but since some women later ran businesses of their own, they must have learned how to do essential arithmetic, too.

Our understanding of justice in ancient Egypt is patchy. We do know, however, that Ma'at—the ideal of justice and balance, as symbolized by the goddess of that name—was important. We also know it was against the law to steal. An ordinary case of theft would be investigated first by local police and officials, who were allowed to beat and torture suspects. If the case couldn't be resolved, other officials became involved. Punishments could include beating, branding, forced labor, or mutilation. The ultimate judge in the land was the pharaoh, and stealing from the pharaoh himself (or from a temple or royal tomb) was an especially serious crime. It could be considered treason, and the thief could be punished by death.

Finally, I should note that there really was a Director of the Royal Loincloths. There was also a Director of Wigmakers, a Lord of the Royal Wardrobe, and a Chief of the Scented Oils and Pastes for Rubbing His Majesty's Body. Egyptian palaces were full of people with remarkable—and often very long—titles.

A Note About Sources

There are many, many books about ancient Egypt. The ones that were most useful to me as I wrote this mystery were:

Anton Gill, *Ancient Egyptians: The Kingdom of the Pharaohs Brought to Life* (London: HarperCollins, 2003)

Jaromir Malek, *The Cat in Ancient Egypt* (London: British Museum Press, 1993)

Garry J. Shaw, *The Pharaoh: Life at Court and on Campaign* (London: Thames & Hudson, 2012)

Steven Snape, *The Complete Cities of Ancient Egypt* (London: Thames & Hudson, 2014)

Neal Spencer, *The Gayer-Anderson Cat* (London: British Museum Press, 2007)

Here are some recommended books about ancient Egypt for young readers:

Crispin Boyer, *Everything Ancient Egypt* (Washington, D.C.: National Geographic Children's Books, 2012)

George Hart, *Ancient Egypt* (New York: DK Eyewitness Books, 2014)

Dominique Navarro, *Egypt's Wildlife: Past and Present* (Cairo: American University in Cairo Press, 2016)

Lesley Sims, *Visitors' Guide to Ancient Egypt* (Tulsa, Oklahoma: EDC Publishing, 2001)

Marcia Williams, *Ancient Egypt: Tales of Gods and Pharaohs* (Somerville, Massachusetts: Candlewick, 2013)

Acknowledgments

I'm a lucky author to have Sarah Horne illustrating this book. Her work is the cat's meow. Thank you, Sarah!

I'm grateful to my jewel of an editor, Sally Morgridge, and to all the wonderful people at Holiday House, especially Mary Cash, Terry Borzumato-Greenberg, Amy Toth, Mora Couch, and Kelly Loughman. Big thanks also go to my lovely agent, Sara Crowe, and to everyone at Pippin.

A tip of the whiskers and warmest thanks to the writers and organizers of Charney 2015, where I first had the idea for this book. Special thanks to Paula Harrison and Kit Sturtevant, two terrific writers who critiqued an early draft.

I'm grateful to Rachel Ridout for checking the initial submission and to Sylvia Atalla for guidance on pronunciation. I'd also like to thank copyeditor Barbara Perris, who handled Ra with marvelous care.

This book wouldn't exist if it weren't for the British Museum, source of inspiration and delight.

Thanks, hugs, and cat-kisses to my two most dedicated readers: my daughter and my husband. You are my purr-fect family!

Read on for a sneak peek at
Ra and Khepri's next case!

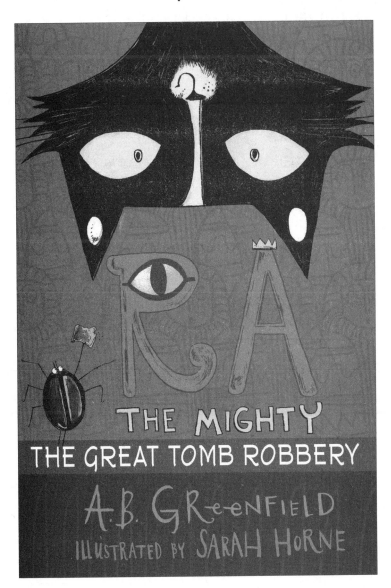

RA

THE MIGHTY
THE GREAT TOMB ROBBERY

A.B. GReeNFIELD
ILLUSTRATED BY SARAH HORNE

CHAPTER I

Pampering

I'm not hard to please. Ask anyone. But when you're covered with fur and you've spent two full days traveling up the Nile under the fiery summer sun, you expect a little pampering. Especially if you're Ra the Mighty, Pharaoh's Cat.

Luckily, I travel with my own special pampering crew. We reached the palace at Thebes at dawn, and they whisked me away to Pharaoh's private garden. There they offered me a cushion and a snack of spiced ibex while they unpacked their brushes and perfumes.

I was on my third chunk of ibex when a tiny voice piped up from somewhere between my ears. "Ra? You're not really

going to wear perfume, are you?"

"Of course I am," I said. "I know you haven't been to Thebes before, but it's a noble city with high standards. Trust me, it's a glamorous place. I always wear perfume here."

"Then I'm getting off." My fur rippled, and my buddy Khepri bounded onto the stones by my cushion. For a scarab beetle, he's pretty quick on his feet. It must be all that dung-rolling he does.

"Suit yourself." I snarfed up the last chunk of ibex. "But if you ask me, a little perfume wouldn't hurt you, Khepri. Anyone who spends as much time with dung as you do—"

"Dung smells *wonderful*," Khepri protested.

"I beg to differ." I rolled onto my side as the attendants came forward with their brushes. "You won't catch me smelling like a dung pile, ever."

Not for the first time, I was glad my attendants couldn't understand a word Khepri and I were saying. (Humans never do.)

"You're missing out, Ra," Khepri said earnestly.

"I'm not missing a thing," I said. "Jasmine, lily, myrrh—that's what I call perfume."

"Blech." Khepri backed up until he was a safe distance away from the perfume bottles. "I think I'll go explore the palace."

"Sure," I said, yawning. I bent my head

and allowed the attendants to smooth the fur between my ears. (That's the bit Khepri always rucks up.) "You go on ahead. I'll catch up with you later."

"Great," Khepri chirped. "By then, maybe I'll have a new case for us."

I lifted my head. "Oh, Khepri. Not that again." We had solved exactly one mystery together, and I had thought that was plenty. But Khepri had other ideas.

"You need to be more open, Ra," Khepri insisted. "I keep bringing you cases, and you keep turning them down. The case of the missing loaves—"

"They weren't missing," I said. "The baker's assistant miscounted. He's never been good with numbers."

"—and the case of the mysterious stranger—"

"I told you: it was the Assyrian ambassador."

"—and the case of the disappearing dung pile—"

"Khepri, I draw the line at dung." I twisted so that the attendants could brush my tummy. "We're Great Detectives, my friend. We require a Great Mystery, not some piddling little nothing of a case. When a Great Mystery appears, then I'll get involved. But not before."

"Well, I'd be okay with a Small Mystery," Khepri said. "Even a Very Small Mystery."

"You're right, Khepri," said a brisk voice behind us. "Even a Very Small Mystery would be good for Ra."

It was our fellow Great Detective, Miu—kitchen cat extraordinaire. I flipped over and braced myself. Miu is a terrific friend, brave and loyal, but she has this strange idea that the life I lead doesn't build character. (Honestly! Everyone knows that Pharaoh's Cat is born with oodles of character. He hardly needs more.)

I greeted her with a ripple of my whiskers. "I thought you were going to stay on the boat and search for stowaway rats."

"Job done," Miu reported with pride. She rubbed a paw over her torn ear, clearing a cobweb away. "How about you, Ra? Have you accomplished anything since we arrived?"

"I've accomplished a snack," I said.

Miu's whiskers twitched. "That doesn't count."

"Sure it counts." I yawned and went floppy again. The attendants were getting to my tail—my favorite bit.

"No matter how many times I see this, I can't believe it," Miu said, watching. "Cats are supposed to clean themselves, Ra. Like this." She started licking her hindquarters.

I shut my eyes. "Uggh. I'm willing to give myself a quick touch-up here and there. But a serious cleaning? Licking dirt off with my *tongue*? You've got to be kidding me."

"We're cats," Miu said. "That's what we do."

"Not Pharaoh's Cat," I insisted. "I have people for that. See?" The attendants gave me one last stroke, then picked up their perfume bottles.

"Perfume?" Miu looked scandalized. "Ra, that's a step too far."

"This is Thebes, Miu. You haven't really seen the place yet, but that's how they do things around here." As the attendants rubbed their perfumes into my fur, I sniffed at the air with a glad sigh. "Mmmm . . . this

is my favorite. Jasmine with overtones of
lotus."

Miu wrinkled her nose. "Somebody needs
to save you from yourself, Ra."

I waved a languid paw. "I'm fine. No saving needed."

Miu ignored me. She's a very strong-
minded cat. "Khepri, we're going to have to
intervene. We need to find a mystery for Ra,
and fast."

Khepri clicked his forelegs in agreement. "Aye, aye!"

I had other ideas. Duty done, the attendants bowed and stepped back. I rose from my cushion, gave myself a good stretch, then strutted toward the door.

"Ra, where are you going?" Miu asked.

Khepri scuttled after me. "Yes, where?"

I paused at the doorway. "It's a mystery," I told them, and bounded away.

CHAPTER 2

Great Pharaoh's Cat

Pampered or not, I can move fast when I want to. By the time Miu and Khepri caught up with me, I'd reached my destination: the side courtyard.

Khepri hopped off Miu and clambered onto me. "What's going on, Ra?"

"Tell you in a minute," I said.

Pharaoh stood with his guards arrayed around him. His gold-embroidered tunic shone in the sun. Before him, bowing low, was the Vizier of the South, the top official in Thebes. As Pharaoh's deputy, he was responsible for managing the palace, collecting taxes, and enforcing the law in his domain.

Seeing me, Pharaoh broke off his conversation with the Vizier. "Ra, you look

The VIZIER

magnificent. Vizier, you remember my cat?"

"Indeed I do." Turning toward me, the Vizier bowed still more deeply. "Ra the Mighty, Lord of the Powerful Paw, Great Pharaoh's Cat, how very good to welcome you again to the royal palace at Thebes."

The bow was a nice touch, but I wasn't fooled. The Vizier had never been a fan of mine, not since the day I attacked his wig and chewed it up in front of the whole court. (It looked like a rat, I swear.) I was only a frisky kitten then, so you'd think he'd forgive and forget. But he hasn't.

When Pharaoh wasn't looking, the Vizier curled his lip at me. I curled mine right back, showing my pointy teeth.

Pharaoh smiled down on us both. "We are glad you're pleased to see Ra, Vizier. Especially as you'll be spending the whole day together."

The Vizier choked. "The wh-whole day? O Ruler of Rulers, I am not worthy."

"Possibly not," Pharaoh agreed, "but we need you to bring Ra to the Valley of the Kings today. He is to pose for the artists who are working on our tomb. They will create a wall painting of him and a sculpture, both as large as life."

"There," I said to Miu and Khepri. "Now you see why I wanted a proper brushing."

Miu looked confused. "You're wearing perfume for your *tomb*?"

"It's all part of the package," I told her. "It sets a distinctive tone."

She rubbed a paw against her nose. "It certainly does."

"I've always wanted to see the Valley of the Kings," Khepri said wistfully, high on the top of my head. "That's where the pharaohs are buried in their pyramids, right?"

"You need to keep up with the times," I told him. "Nobody builds pyramids anymore, Khepri. Too old-fashioned. Too obvious. Might as well put up a huge sign saying 'Robbers, here's the treasure.' That's why the pharaohs switched to the Valley of the Kings. It's guarded, it's private, and it's only for royals. They build the tombs into the cliffs, and once they're sealed, most people can't even guess where the entrances are."

"So there's nothing to see?" Khepri sounded disappointed.

"Oh, there's plenty of desert cliffs, if you like that sort of thing. They're quite majestic, if you catch them in the right light. And you could probably peek in at Pharaoh's tomb-in-progress—"

"Ooooh." Khepri perked up. "Really?"

"I don't see why not. And while you're there, we can look at mine, too. I can't remember what I've told you about it—"

"Pharaoh designed it," Khepri chirped.

"It's going to have a chamber connected to his," Miu put in.

"And walls patterned in carnelian and lapis lazuli—"

"And paintings of your favorite pool—"

"And a gilded cat bed—"

"With a jeweled cushion—"

"And little clay servants—"

"To brush your fur—"

"And a cat-shaped sarcophagus," Khepri finished.

"Do I really talk about it so much?" I said.

"Oh, no," said Khepri.

"Oh, yes," said Miu.

"Well, who can blame me?" I said happily. "It's going to be quite extraordinary. And did I mention the snacks?" Merely thinking about them made me lick my lips: wooden boxes packed to the brim with mummified quail and ibex and mutton and antelope. "I won't go hungry in the afterlife, that's for sure."

As far as I'm concerned, that's the whole point of a tomb. A gilded cat bed and a jeweled cushion are nice accessories, and I'm fond of the clay servants that will wait on me for all eternity, but it's the food I care about most—and not just because I'm a bit of a gourmet. The priests say you need two things for a good afterlife: a properly preserved mummy, and enough food to sustain your spirit. If you don't have those, then you can kiss the hereafter good-bye.

"Of course, everything's a work in progress at the moment," I reminded Miu and Khepri. "That's why I need to go pose."

Khepri was practically bouncing between my ears. "Ra, can I come with you?"

"Sure," I said. "You can entertain me while they draw. You come too, Miu."

She scratched her side with her hind paw. "I'll pass."

"How can you say no, Miu?" Chittering with excitement, Khepri danced by my ear. "A whole day in the Valley of the Kings— wow! We can go exploring, Ra. And maybe we'll find a Great Mystery. Something spooky, maybe—or even buried treasure."

"Sorry, Khepri. I'll be too busy posing." He looked so disappointed that I added, "But you can look around by yourself if you want to."

Khepri looked down at his tiny forelegs. "I won't get very far on my own."

I couldn't deny it. Scarabs are small, and the Valley of the Kings is vast.

Miu sighed. "Never mind, Khepri. If you want to go exploring, I'll take you."

Khepri looked up. "But you said you weren't coming."

Miu regarded him fondly. "I changed my mind."

To be continued . . .